"You have no idea what I want, Cali Ellis." He felt his control careen wildly to the point of no return.

"You claim to love your work. Yet you're leaving it. I don't think you know what you want, John McShane."

He tugged her hand off the doorknob and pressed it to his chest. "Feel that?" He could feel the thumping beat himself, could hear it drumming inside his ears. "I know what I want."

Before she could speak, he yanked her hand up, pressed her fingers to his temple. "In here, I know what's best. For you. For the team. And, by default, for me."

He tugged her hand back to his chest. "But in here I'm lost. I have no guidelines for following what I feel. As a rule, I try not to feel anything in here."

"Is that so wrong?" she asked, her voice a bare rasp. "Since when is feeling wrong?"

"Since I took on a job where 'feeling' with your head keeps you alive and feeling with your heart gets you dead. And if you're lucky, you're the only one to die. I like what I do. My work satisfies me."

"Then why are you leaving?"

He lowered his mouth. A whisper away from her lips, he said, "Because right now I can only think with my heart."

Cali had no handy excuse for why she accepted his gentle entry willingly, why she didn't struggle when he pulled her hand to his shoulder and slid his around her waist, why she moved fluidly when he tugged her closer, or sighed at the way he fitted too perfectly against her.

WHAT ARE *LOVESWEPT* ROMANCES?

They are stories of true romance and touching emotion. We believe those two very important ingredients are constants in our highly sensual and very believable stories in the LOVE-SWEPT line. Our goal is to give you, the reader, stories of consistently high quality that may sometimes make you laugh, sometimes make you cry, but are always fresh and creative and contain many delightful surprises within their pages.

Most romance fans read an enormous number of books. Those they truly love, they keep. Others may be traded with friends and soon forgotten. We hope that each LOVESWEPT romance will be a treasure—a "keeper." We will always try to publish

LOVE STORIES YOU'LL NEVER FORGET
BY AUTHORS YOU'LL ALWAYS REMEMBER

The Editors

Loveswept ® 831

SILENT WARRIOR

DONNA KAUFFMAN

BANTAM BOOKS
NEW YORK · TORONTO · LONDON · SYDNEY · AUCKLAND

SILENT WARRIOR
A Bantam Book / April 1997

ISBN 0-553-44539-1

Published simultaneously in the United States and Canada

Bantam Books are published by Bantam Books, a division of Bantam Doubleday Dell Publishing Group, Inc. Its trademark, consisting of the words "Bantam Books" and the portrayal of a rooster, is Registered in U.S. Patent and Trademark Office and in other countries. Marca Registrada. Bantam Books, 1540 Broadway, New York, New York 10036.

PRINTED IN THE UNITED STATES OF AMERICA

OPM   10 9 8 7 6 5 4 3 2 1

This book is dedicated to
Jean Brashear.

There aren't too many people in the
world who understand the true
meaning of friendship.
You, Supreme Babette, could teach a
graduate course.
Thank you for being there.

ONE

John McShane walked slowly up the crushed-shell path to the small bungalow. He paused on the front steps. What in the hell was Cali doing in this godforsaken, bug-infested place? The surrounding Caribbean jungle was fighting to reclaim the narrow porch and winning the battle handily. He shoved at a heavy, tangled trail of bougainvillea that cascaded off the porch roof like a lava flow, ducked under the rest, and made his way to the screen door.

Through the saggy mesh he could see well-worn hardwood floors and blank, white walls. There was no furniture in the front room, just a ceiling fan slogging through the humid air. No Cali either.

How long had she been there?

Ten years had evaporated like mist when he'd seen the name at the bottom of the short note he'd received two weeks earlier.

I hate to ask anything more of you. I promised I never would. But it's important. It's about Nathan. I'm in trouble. Please help me. You're the only one I trust.

Cali Ellis

P.S. I'm sorry.

No return address. The postmark had been too blotted to read. His only clue to her whereabouts was an old honeymoon picture of herself and Nathan that she'd enclosed with the note. It had been taken in front of this bungalow. He'd seen the photo before. In a frame on her nightstand.

Cali and Nathan's courtship had been brief, but no one who had laid eyes on the young couple ever doubted the intensity and depth of their love.

He fingered the photo in his pocket. He'd made himself stare at it repeatedly. Whether the act was a test of his feelings or penance, he wasn't sure. Probably both.

The photo was a little more than a decade old. Ten years seemed like a lifetime ago in his mind, but only yesterday in his heart.

So there he was, half a world away, having left his job in the hands of others at a time when they needed him badly. Of course, the team always needed him badly. That was why he'd agreed to join them.

Known as Delgado's Dirty Dozen, even though there were only four members remaining, the specially trained squad handled various delicate assignments for the United States government that fell outside the boundaries of other intelligence organizations. Usually well outside.

It was the one kind of need he knew he could fulfill. And with his former boss, Seve Delgado, gone and the rest of them facing the difficulty of rebuilding the team, now was the worst time to abandon them. But here he was. Because she trusted him.

Hadn't she learned anything?

He rapped on the screen door a little harder than necessary. It rattled against the frame.

"I'm around back," came a yell.

Her voice was strong, no-nonsense, the words more a command than a welcome. John smiled despite himself. She hadn't changed.

His expression sobered as he ducked off the porch and wove his way through the overgrown path leading around the side of the cottage. For someone who claimed to be in danger, dragging him all over the globe with only a hastily scribbled note, she sure as hell wasn't being very cautious. That was not the Cali Stanfield Ellis he had known.

He turned the corner and stopped in his tracks. She was in the garden, although the term sounded a bit formal for the flower- and weed-choked hill slanting steeply upward from the back door.

On her knees, bent over a thriving poinsettia bush, she looked . . . golden. Her platinum hair was still short with loose curls and as unruly as he remembered. Clad in white shorts and a ragged red T-shirt, she looked strong and capable and somehow soft and inviting at the same time. His heart knotted. He cursed silently.

"Almost done, Eudora," she said without looking up.

"For someone in trouble you sure as hell aren't hiding out too well." He hadn't intended to begin their reunion so bluntly. But then Cali had always had a way of making him do things he hadn't intended.

She gasped, wobbled, caught herself, then pushed to a stand, raking her hair from her face as she turned to him.

"You came," she whispered.

She was thirty feet away and yet those clear green eyes of hers cut straight through him. Straight through ten years of living through each today and ignoring all the yesterdays. Straight through to the soul he'd been pretending he didn't have.

"You asked me to," he said simply. He stepped toward her. "Did you think I'd ignore your message?"

She wiped her hands on her shorts, heedless of the soil and grime now marking the white cotton. "I wasn't even sure you'd get it. It's been so long. I didn't know if—I wasn't sure—" She cut off her uncustomary stammering, and just stared at him.

He let her, not too proud to take a few much-needed seconds to regain his composure. However, it gave him way too much leeway to return the favor, to let himself be reminded of things he'd thought long forgotten. Fool.

He'd spent the long, globe-hopping hours to Martinique telling himself he was just helping an old friend—the *wife* of an old friend and former partner to be exact—that the emotions she had roiled in him a decade before had been long since buried and put to rest.

"You look good, John." She stepped closer, running her sharp-eyed gaze over him. "Playing super-secret spy always did agree with you, though." She took another step.

Don't touch me. The tinge of desperation in the thought darkened his mood. Cali was a hands-on kind of person. It was what had dragged him under the last time. He braced himself.

She stopped right in front of him. He swallowed his sigh of relief when she put her hands on her hips. *Pathetic, McShane. That's what you are.*

"Leaner, but rangy," she said. She looked up into his face, the half-foot difference in their heights further underscored by the hiking boots he wore and her bare feet.

Her toenails were painted red like the flowers she'd been tending . . . or taming. He had no idea when he'd noticed that. He couldn't look away from her face. She had freckles on her nose. Her cheeks were pink from the sun. Her hair was plastered to her forehead and neck. Her mouth was puffy and soft from the heat.

He looked away.

"I'm sorry," she said quietly.

He jerked his gaze back to her. "What for?"

"Dragging you halfway around the world. Playing on your feelings about Nathan to get you to help me.

You're obviously angry at me, and I don't blame you one bit."

Angry? That emotion was solely self-directed. "I'm not here for Nathan."

That seemed to surprise her. She blinked once, then backed away when he continued to stare silently at her. Finally she turned and walked back to the path she'd been clearing when he'd found her.

Yes, he thought. *Turn away from it, Cali. It's what I've been doing for ten years. Don't look too closely. There's no tragedy to provide a convenient shield for me this time.*

Lord, if she ever knew . . .

Had she ever known? No. That question had been asked and answered just as instantly and assuredly ten years earlier. He was a trained professional in masking his emotions, even new, raw, painful ones. One of his teammates, T. J. Delahaye, called the Dirty Dozen silent warriors. But even he was only human. So why in the hell was he there tempting fate—and himself—again?

"Whatever your reasons, I'm glad you did. Thank you." She scooped up the poinsettias she'd cut.

He had to turn away. She looked too good, standing there in the shimmering heat, arms loaded with decadent red-leaved plants that were supposed to remind him of cold winter holidays but looked impossibly tropical and seductive now.

"Why don't we go inside and sit down." He began to make his way back down the path. "You can fill me in on the situation."

He felt her hesitation. "Yes, I guess we should."

He took another step but stilled when she caught up to him and put her hand on his arm. He didn't move away.

She immediately let go. "I just wanted to say you could come in the back way."

It was a hell of a time to discover he was a coward. In almost fifteen years of intelligence work he'd faced down cold-blooded killers, had ended the careers and occasionally the lives of a number of them, had more than once put his body in the path of a bullet to prevent its hitting its target—said target usually human and under his temporary protection. That was his job. He'd done it all without an instant's hesitation. That instant was often the only margin between life and death. His.

Right at that moment he'd have rather stepped in front of an entire round of bullets than turn around and look into Cali's eyes again.

Mere seconds had elapsed when he turned, but he wondered what his hesitation would cost him. One look at her and he knew his safety margin this time was nonexistent.

"If it helps, this isn't easy for me either," she said.

He almost smiled at the defiant undertone lacing her quiet words. That was Cali. Even in the most tense and horrific circumstances she managed to retain her sense of self. He knew, he'd been there to witness it firsthand. He shoved those memories aside.

"Then I suggest we stop wasting time." He worked to remove the hard edge from his tone.

"From the brevity of your note I gather you don't have much of it."

They pushed through the back screen door. There was a small warped wooden table surrounded by four mismatched chairs.

She waved a hand. "Not exactly paradise as I remembered it." Her dry humor didn't ease the tension.

John did not want to think about why she'd been here ten years before. He pulled out the sturdiest chair and sat down while Cali put the cut flowers in a heavy, chipped ceramic vase. She started to set it on the table, but left the lush centerpiece by the sink. One less shield between them.

"You want some bottled water?" she asked. "A beer?"

"Water sounds good."

It wasn't until she sat across from him, fingering the condensation on her bottle, that he realized she'd been playing for time.

"I'm sorry I make you uncomfortable," he said. "But you did ask me to come."

She stilled, then pulled her hands into her lap. "That's not it."

"You said this had to do with Nathan." He didn't want to delve into awkward territory any more than she did. "He's been gone a decade. What could he have done that would come back to haunt you now?"

She looked up, holding his gaze more assuredly. She was focused; in control. But she always had been where Nathan was concerned. It was why he'd purposely given her the mental foothold. Anything to get her mind off of him and their particular shared past.

"It's pretty complicated. I don't have all the pieces yet."

"Give me what you've got."

She smiled. "I still can't quite believe you're here."

Neither can I. He frowned. "I haven't done anything yet." He didn't want her gratitude. Not now or ever again.

"You're willing to help. It's more than I expected."

He sighed in frustration. "Cali, I told you a long time ago that if you ever needed anything—"

She held her hand up. "And I told you—promised you—that I'd never ask you for anything again. I meant it. If this weren't so serious, if I had anyone else to turn to, I'd never have contacted you again. I know I'm exploiting the hell out of your strong sense of duty. Just as I know you don't want to be here."

I wish. He ignored the twinge in his heart. He'd decided when he'd left her in that hospital room ten years earlier that he'd never see her again. He'd had no choice, as he'd seen the situation. So her honest declaration now shouldn't bother him. It was the same one he'd made to himself many many times.

She folded her arms. "So just take my thanks and deal with it, McShane."

"Yes, ma'am."

She eased some of the defiance out of her posture

and her tone. "You can't imagine what this means to me."

"I'm trying not to imagine anything. I'd rather have facts. It's not like you to stall. Spit it out, Cali."

She straightened. "And it's just like you to turn gratitude and sincere thanks into a fault. I already owe you a debt I could never—"

"Stop. Don't go there, Cali." His tone was just as hard and cold as she accused him of being. He didn't care. "I'm here. Let's let the rest go, okay?"

She glared at him, but finally raised a hand in resignation. "Fine. But I want you to know one other thing."

"Why I'm here perhaps?"

She ignored his sarcasm. "If after you hear me out you don't want to help me, say so. I'll understand. Though any other path you could steer me to would be greatly appreciated." Her temper drained as fast as it had boiled over. Her shoulders rounded again. "You really are my last hope, John."

Then you really are in trouble. His eyes were gritty from lack of sleep and an excess of repressed emotion. He curled his fingers into a fist to keep from rubbing at them. "I'll do what I can, Cali. Now enough of this. Tell me."

She took a slow swallow of water. He worked hard not to push her any further, but his patience was riding a very thin line and what control he had left was close to gone.

Then she looked directly at him. John saw in her eyes something he hadn't seen since that night ten years earlier when she'd called him, panicked, unable to track down her father, who was en route to California for Nathan's funeral.

The night she'd lost Nathan's baby.

He saw fear. Vulnerability. Emotions he knew she kept well managed and hidden from public view.

But he'd seen them and more. Cali Stanfield Ellis had pride, too much of it sometimes. Considering her background, which included being the only daughter of one of the United States' most revered and honored ambassadors, as well as an acclaimed developer of leading-edge computer technology, it was understandable.

And in a span of less than a week she'd been robbed of most all of it. He'd seen her completely undone by what life had handed her. It had handed her a horrific burden that would have crumbled most women. Married less than six months, it hadn't been a slow descent either, but viciously ripped from her with a two-fisted yank.

He'd been the sole witness to her private destruction.

He curled his fingers tightly around the bottle to keep from reaching for her hand.

To do what, John? his mind queried. *Help her? The way you helped her last time? Offering heartfelt, but ultimately worthless advice about how unfair her double loss had been?*

How much had it really helped her to have him sit by her side day and night, telling her he was there for her no matter what, that Nathan had not only been his partner but his friend, and death didn't keep him from standing by his friends?

Had he really helped her when every single second of that devastating time in her life he'd sat there knowing that, more than anything in the world, he'd wanted her to belong to him?

Yeah. A real knight in shining armor he was.

He downed the rest of his water, then plopped the bottle back on the table harder than was necessary. She flinched.

He didn't feel bad about that either. Not one bit. He was a son-of-a-bitch. She'd told him that herself. She'd been right. Ten years hadn't changed that. Ask anyone who'd worked with him.

"Who's after you, Cali, and why?"

"Your boss," she shot back, feeding off his frustrated energy. "The U.S. government." Her green eyes flashed bright and hard.

Anything to extinguish the pain he still saw there, he thought. "Your old boss too," he reminded her. "And Nathan's."

"Yeah, well, it turns out they have a rather undesirable retirement program. Instead of an engraved gold watch you get an unmarked lead bullet."

Internal battles were instantly forgotten. John leaned forward and gripped her forearm. "Someone shot at you?"

She looked first at his hand, then at him. He let her go.

"Several someones, yes," she replied.

She absently rubbed her arm where he'd touched

her. He doggedly kept his attention on her face. "What do you have that they want? Information? What are you into these days? Still doing new tech development in decoding? Did you go back to work for Uncle Sam?"

Keeping track of her over the years would have been easy. He hadn't done so. Only now did he realize how foolish he'd been to believe that proved anything.

"I freelance," she said. "I have since Nathan died. Most of my clients are L.A.-based like me. Mostly cyber technology. All civilian. After we married, I never took on government contracts. That was Nathan's department. He died so soon after that, he never got very far into the contracts he'd signed with them."

"Is that what has come back to haunt you? One of Nathan's specialized projects?"

"Yes. You know how good he was. Nathan, the technology wizard. The man who could take the most archaic PC and turn it into a tool of global espionage. You remember the way he ferreted out information. It was mind-boggling. We both knew he'd have no trouble getting civilian work, and he didn't. He hadn't been gone from the Blue Circle long, we hadn't even been married a few weeks, and the offers were already coming in."

John wasn't at all surprised. He had worked with Nathan closely for several years, doing highly sensitive work for an adjunct branch of the CIA known as the Blue Circle, the name referring to the global range of their assignments. The Dirty Dozen handled similar, if tougher, assignments. They just weren't as tightly supervised. Then, as now, John was strategist and lead coordinator of the missions assigned to them. Nathan had been just what Cali had described him, the techno wizard.

"Whatever the assignment," John said, "I can't believe that with the technological strides we've made in the last ten years, anything he was working on then could be that sensitive now."

Cali snorted and crossed her arms. "Maybe I shouldn't feel so appallingly naive. I thought the same thing. Until I came home from work one afternoon about a month ago."

"Your place had been searched?"

"At some earlier point I'm sure it had been. I never knew it then. But this time they were far more thorough. They simply took it all with them."

"What?" If the sudden tightness in his voice fazed her, she didn't show it.

"Emptied it out. Didn't leave so much as a paper clip or roll of toilet paper behind."

Tension crawled through his muscles at the same time adrenaline pulsed into his bloodstream. He welcomed both even as he hated the cause.

"All I have is what I stored in my safety-deposit box, which is next to nothing. It was my mother's. Father set it up years ago. After she died, I just never got around to getting one of my own." She blew out a long breath and raked her hand through her hair. When she looked at him again, the pain was edging back into her eyes. "They took it all, John. All my pictures, everything that was personal to me. All gone."

"Start at the beginning." *Think business, McShane. Not haunted green eyes.* "Leave nothing out."

She sighed again, but pulled herself together. "Nathan's first contract came in right after he left the Blue Circle. The security clearance required was extensive."

"But he already had top clearance."

"That's what I thought. They even went over my background and security clearance. I know, I know," she said, waving him silent. "Between being Ambassador Stanfield's daughter and doing some top security clearance work myself, you'd think I was clear too. But they—"

"Who's 'they' in this case, Cali? Which branch hired him?"

She smiled but there was no humor in it. "That's just it, I didn't even know. Neither did Nathan. It went through several channels before getting to him. His contact was actually someone high up in the Blue Circle chain of command."

"What was the contract?"

"To write a computer program, but I have no idea for what. They made it very clear I wasn't to be told anything. Even after he underwent the clearance they weren't too keen on Nathan working at home. They offered—if you could call it that—to set him up in an office."

"Where? D.C.?"

"No, we could have stayed in California."

"Well funded, whoever they are."

"Yes, we both realized that. Even with the Circle contact and apparent approval, Nathan was suspicious. But the dollar figure attached to the contract was too good to pass up."

"He never struck me as the type to have a price."

Cali bristled. "He didn't. But the highly mysterious nature of the job intrigued him. The money would allow him to pick and choose what clients he took on as a civilian. There was also an implied offer of other work for this group if they approved of his work on this project. For someone just starting out, even someone with his government contacts, it was too lucrative to pass up. And I'll admit that both of us wanted to know more about what was really going on, and we knew that the only way to find out was for Nathan to take the job."

"So he talked to you anyway. About the job."

She nodded. "Even Nathan understood the rationale for secrecy. And to protect me more than anything, we had decided that he would share with me only what he felt he could."

"What did he tell you? Did he leave any notes?" John leaned forward. "I want to see everything you have on this."

She smiled wearily. "You haven't changed, McShane. Once a bulldog, always a bulldog."

"It's why you asked me here, isn't it?"

She glanced away, her frame looking suddenly frail to him. The image was so at odds with the Cali

Ellis he'd known, he felt his nerves string even tighter. Struggling with emotions was something John McShane never had to worry about. He was a champ at tucking them away. Only once in his life had they roiled to the surface and threatened to drown him. The woman across the table had been responsible then too.

He wouldn't let it happen again.

"It's been ten years, Cali. Surely talking about Nathan's death shouldn't make you fall apart."

Her gaze swung fiercely to his. "You don't know everything. And I don't fall apart." When he opened his mouth, she braced her palms on the table. "Don't, McShane," she warned him. "I didn't go there. Don't you either."

Keeping her on the defensive helped. He should be ashamed. He was, but he didn't back down. He was too busy keeping his head above the tide to worry about the life preserver he'd chosen. "You're the one who wanted to talk about it. It was a tough time, Cali. Worse than anyone should have to deal with. No one blamed you for falling apart."

"*You* did."

She'd caught him off guard with that one, and he was certain his expression reflected it. "What in the hell gave you that idea?"

"Gee, I don't know, McShane. Maybe it was the hostile way you treated me. I lost a baby and a husband in the span of one week, and you patted me on the head, told me how sorry you were, then all but ordered me to get over it and on with my life. You didn't nudge, you shoved."

"Someone had to." His tone was no more gentle now than it had been then.

She pushed from her chair and paced the small room. Her skin shone with perspiration, her T-shirt clung to her breasts and stuck against her stomach. The same stomach she'd clutched in agony as blood and a life had ebbed from her body. He'd never felt so incredibly, horribly helpless. He'd never been so angry. At the senseless injustice. At himself for feeling sorry for himself when she was the only one who deserved sympathy.

He hardened his mind to the memories of what had followed that awful night. And later . . . in the hospital. What had happened between them had been a fight for survival. Only he knew his methods had been every bit as much for himself as for her.

"You needed to deal with what happened and get on with your life, to function in the present," he said to her retreating back. His gaze dropped to her shorts and the long legs that showed beneath the ragged hem. Swearing silently, he looked back to his empty bottle. "You weren't exactly the type to take a pat on the hand and soft words of comfort."

"I think that was understandable."

Understandable. Yes, John thought, excruciatingly understandable. "No one else was getting through to you," he said, persisting even as he questioned the wisdom of not just letting it go. "I did the only thing I knew to do. If you were mad at me, at least you had a focus and a vent for all your anger."

She just snorted. That stung. Even though he knew he'd had the bedside manner of a tiger with a thorn in its paw.

Cali paced the length of the room twice, then suddenly halted in mid-stride. With a brief sigh, she slumped back against the counter, arms folded. She looked at John, her expression tired but not defeated. "I know why you did what you did," she said quietly. "I knew it then. And you were right. I wasn't any good to anyone the way I was, least of all myself. If you recall, I did finally thank you for it."

Yes, she had. John heard her last words to him as clearly as if she'd just repeated them. The doctors had wanted to send her home for several days after they'd finally stopped the hemorrhaging and stabilized her. But she'd lingered with one complaint or another, so unlike herself that her own family had been at a loss as to how to handle her. He'd been with her during the worst of it, and he knew she was beginning to regret his having seen that side of her. Defeated and embarrassed, despite the understanding though somewhat claustrophobia-inducing support of her father, she'd sunk into a depression.

John had known that someone needed to shake her up a bit and get her focused on something other than the trauma she'd just endured. He'd elected himself for the job. Making her angry, and focusing that anger at him, had helped him deal with the guilt of his unwanted feelings for her too.

He'd gone into her hospital room that day and bullied her, pushed her, hating the pain and betrayal he'd seen in her eyes. She'd finally lost her temper, coming out of the numb, almost trancelike shell she'd lapsed into, yelling at him.

"You tell me you miss him, too, that you understand, but you don't," she'd yelled. *"You never have. Underneath all your nice, sympathetic words you're just a coldhearted son-of-a-bitch. You say you feel things, but there is no evidence of them on your face. Not once have I seen even a glimmer of feeling in your eyes. The ultimate super-spy, Nathan called you. He admired the hell out of you. I have no idea why. I still don't. You're hard and emotionless. It seems to me to be good at your job you have to feel something, anything. You don't feel, you don't react. You just act.*

"Nathan told me I just didn't understand you. Well, he was right, I don't. I don't know why you're here now when you'd obviously rather be anywhere else. But I'll be damned if I'll lie here and take any more of this abuse from you." She'd eventually wound down, but anger still flashed in her brilliant green eyes when she'd said, *"Now go find me a nurse and get me the hell out of here."*

He'd willingly taken her flaying, silently begging her to give him her worst. He deserved it even as he felt shame for the relief of guilt her well-earned outburst had delivered to him. He'd left her room, arranged her release, and contacted her father to come for her. Then he'd left. Gone back to work. He'd seen it as his only choice.

Only now it seemed a whole lot more like running away.

"Did you ever get the letter I sent you?"

"Yeah," he said. "I got it." And would go to his grave before admitting he still had it. He started to explain why he'd never written back, even though the note hadn't required a response, but she spoke first.

"I meant what I said, John."

"Which time? In the letter or in the hospital room?"

She smiled. It made his chest ache.

"Both, actually. I resented that I needed someone to push me so hard, to make me do what I knew I needed to do. But I also meant what I said to you in that letter. You were Nathan's friend. You honored that by taking care of me through some very rough stuff you didn't have to stick around for. I may not have liked your methods, but I never forgot what you did for me."

"I thought we weren't going to talk about this," he grumbled.

To his further chagrin, her smile widened, reaching her eyes this time. God, she was beautiful. Inside and out.

"I think it was better to get it out of the way," she said. "I know it's awkward. But you're right, it's been long enough now. It shouldn't be so hard to talk about. I couldn't go on, asking for your help again, without at least talking about how we parted last time."

"You said I didn't know everything. Tell me the rest."

Her smile turned a bit sad, acknowledging that he'd just closed the subject.

"I think the meeting Nathan was on his way to the day he died involved this project." She crossed back to the table and sat down, bracing her forearms on the table.

"Meaning what?"

"What I'm saying is that ten years ago Nathan was working on this project and he died. Now the project surfaces, falling into my hands. And now someone wants me dead too."

TWO

Cali looked across the table at the man she'd asked to save her life. What had she been thinking with anyway? Certainly not with what was left of her brain.

Ten years spent building a rock-solid, independent life should have inured her to the overwhelming effect of one John McShane. He was just a man.

Right. And she was just a hacker.

She'd told herself she'd exaggerated the power of his steely reserve, of his rigid, unemotional control. That she'd no longer suffer the irritation of discovering that despite his obvious faults, she'd found herself intrigued by those same traits more than once.

As her father's hostess, she'd held court for princes and rebels with equal ease. Surely one United States super-spy shouldn't throw her. Surely it had been her youth and the circumstances of their initial meeting that had caused her reaction.

A decade later she had to face the truth. She was still intrigued by him.

Had he always been so impossibly rugged? Had his eyes always been that cold, steely gray?

To her further dismay, his intense return scrutiny had her averting her gaze. She watched the condensation trickle down the side of her bottle. The direction of her life seemed as random as the beads of water on the glass. She hated the loss of control more than anything else. Hated that she was about to hand over what little control she had left to anyone, but in particular to this man. Once in a lifetime was enough. Never mind that she'd asked him to take control both times.

And for whatever reason, he'd come. Again. She looked up. Beating herself up with the whys of their past, with guilt over dragging him into her messy life once again, helped no one. She was desperate. She'd figure out how to pay him back later.

"You think his death wasn't an accident," he stated. "You think it's related to what's happening to you now?"

"I have no concrete proof of the connection. But yes, I do," she said. "When you came to our apartment and told me that Nathan had been killed in a car crash, it never occurred to me that it was anything other than an accident. I know you and the Blue Circle investigated it anyway and concurred with that conclusion. But someone in the Blue Circle was also part of the chain of command on the project. So the fact that they found nothing proves nothing."

"He died in a car accident on the way to a meeting, Cali. There was absolutely no evidence of foul play. There was nothing else to investigate. We questioned you on his current projects, and you had no specific information about what he'd been working on. No one we talked to in the Circle knew anything about it. His contact never stepped forward."

"Mighty convenient, don't you think? And neither driver survived. Hard to get a confession from a dead man." She leaned back and crossed her arms, holding his gaze intently.

He stared at her. She waited for the argument. Instead, he asked, "How did the project surface again?"

"It was literally handed back to me. By an insurance company." A fresh rush of frustration pushed at her. "Nathan apparently understood better than he let on just how sensitive the project was. We'd already decided not to discuss particulars for my protection, but he must have felt the need for more insurance. So that was exactly what he did. He insured it."

"The project? Or himself?"

"Himself. But I know it was the project that made him do it."

"Explain."

"He'd received the first payment, an advance based on some preliminary work he'd delivered to them the day before his accident. I didn't know about that. The deal hadn't originally been set up that way. Anyway, as it turns out, he took the money, a substantial sum, and set up a convoluted funding system to pay against a policy he bought to cover himself."

"Sounds like something Nathan would do."

She nodded, surprised at how much comfort there was, even now, in being able to share her past, to share what she had with Nathan, with someone who knew him as she had. She smiled softly. "I'm sure he relished the challenge, despite the concerns that drove him to do it." She sobered. "He died that same day. I was the sole beneficiary. I never saw the policy or got any paperwork on it, so the bank and the insurance company weren't notified of his death. The bank account paid into the policy automatically on a regular basis. It was set up as a ten-year note."

"Which just paid out."

"Exactly."

"And the paperwork generated by all of this?"

"Stored in a safety-deposit box in the same bank, filed automatically by some arrangement he worked out. I was only to be notified of all of this if anything happened to him." She stopped, sighing. "I guess he didn't want to worry me."

If she expected any compassion, she was waiting on the wrong man to deliver it. In a way, that relieved her. It *had* been many years. And though all of this had dredged up a lot of old, buried emotions, grief wasn't one of them. She'd long since come to terms with her losses. What she couldn't deal with was the idea that Nathan's death might not have been accidental.

And she'd let ten years lapse without bringing the killer to justice.

"So you got the money," John said, making some notes in the column of his notebook. "What about the program? You went through his things when he died and—"

"Whatever had been done on each contracted project was turned over to the contracted group. I never did find any work on the Blue Circle project."

"You weren't suspicious, though."

"I had no real reason to be. He'd just started it, as far as I knew. They never contacted me asking for anything. I assumed anything he'd had, he'd turned in. I was dealing with so much at the time, I was more relieved than anything."

John was silent for a moment. She could almost hear the wheels turning. Nathan had often boasted of McShane's almost fanatical persistence in analyzing situations. It was the one thing she'd trusted about him back then. It was the reason she'd given herself for asking him to help her now.

"Okay. So ten years have gone by. The project is—or was—as dead and buried as it's creator."

She flinched. He may have well earned his super-spy reputation. However, his status as a sensitive human being was still up for discussion.

He didn't apologize, though she had no doubt he noticed her reaction. He noticed everything. She worked not to shift in her seat as he continued to stare at her.

"Why are you so sure the insurance payoff ties in with the Blue Circle project?"

"When I found out the policy had been paid for with a direct deposit, I traced the payments with my computer to the bank where he'd set up the account. It was on Grand Cayman. As private as a Swiss account and all the transfers done by wire. Luckily my name was on it as well, or I'd have never cracked it."

He lifted an eyebrow.

"Okay, so maybe I could have. But not legally." When he simply continued to look at her, she sighed and went on. "Anyway, there were two automatic payments on the account. One to the insurance policy and a second one for a safety-deposit box in the same bank."

"The policy papers you mentioned already. Was the program work in there too?"

She shook her head. "But along with the paperwork, there was a diskette. It contained his preliminary notes, the ones for which he'd been paid. I'm assuming he expected to continue putting up-to-date work in there for safekeeping, only he never got any further. Regardless, that ties the insurance policy and the program together."

"There wasn't anything else? Personal notes to you?"

Cali glanced down for a second, then met his even gaze. "There was one other thing. A copy of the picture I sent to you."

"No note on the back?"

She shook her head.

He was silent for a few seconds. She watched him scratch out a few more notes. "How did the feds get involved?" he asked without looking up.

So he was going to ignore the photo. For now, anyway.

"My initial reaction, once I got past the shock of it all, was the same as yours. What good was ten-year-old technology?"

He looked at her. "You tracked down his Circle contact?"

She frowned. "I tried. I stupidly assumed after all this time it was a moot point. But I had information about a program they had contracted and paid for. Given the top security clearance involved, they had the right to know about the existence of more material on the assignment. Technically it was their property."

"Who did you talk to?"

"Well, as you probably know, there is no Blue Circle any longer. It was phased out a few years ago. But since Nathan's commander was retired from the CIA, I figured I could track him down. He had no idea who Nathan's contact might have been. But he gave me the name of a Blue Circle muck-a-muck who was still active in the CIA."

"Is that who took the call, then?"

"Initially, yes. Then I was rerouted to another office. I spoke with a man named Gerald Grimshaw. Deputy director of research technology."

"Never heard of that department."

"Me neither. But I wasn't put off by that. I mean, I

don't think there is any one person, including the director himself, who knows all the offices and personnel that run that monster."

"Did Grimshaw show any undue interest in your news?"

"Actually, no. Not at first anyway. He asked what the program was for. I told him it was classified and that, accordingly, I hadn't looked at it."

"Had you?"

"No, McShane," she said evenly. "I hadn't. I was just going by the written note on the envelope the diskette was in."

"Continue."

She swallowed her irritation at his abrupt manner. He'd come halfway around the world to help her. She could hardly quibble over his rude, less-than-sensitive methods.

"He grilled me on who I was, my background, and so forth," she continued. "I explained everything and told him that I was just trying to get the program to its rightful owner."

"Do you still have the disk?"

"I mailed all of it to Grimshaw."

"A copy?"

She shook her head.

"Cali—"

"Don't lecture me, McShane. I know it was stupid. But I really thought it was more a matter of policy. I didn't think Grimshaw would do more than look at the files and toss it as useless."

"Did you look at the file names at least?"

"Encrypted."

John simply smiled at her.

"Okay, so I looked that far. But I didn't decode it."

His smile vanished. "If you gave them his notes, then why did they come after you?"

"They didn't believe I gave them all I had. They want the whole thing. I was questioned politely but at length by Grimshaw and another agent. They showed up less than forty-eight hours after they received the disk."

"Tipped their hand a bit, I'd say."

Cali nodded. "They were a bit intense. They'd checked me out. I came up clean. I wasn't sure whether they were relieved or disappointed about that. My work history interested them a great deal. Nothing I said convinced them I hadn't decrypted the information."

"Couldn't they?"

She smiled then. "Apparently not. I did offer to help them out." Her smile widened. "For a price."

John smiled in return. Cali felt her pulse speed up even as she was perversely irritated. Sharing even a small moment of connection with McShane was disconcerting. She almost liked him better when he was being dictatorial.

"They didn't take you up on it."

"No. They took everything I had instead."

John fell silent, his attention shifted back to the notepad in front of him. He scribbled some more, then studied what he'd compiled. Cali remained silent, doubting he'd answer any questions she asked at this point. He tapped his pen against the paper. "You have no idea what he was working on? Not even a hint?"

"None. The file names didn't reveal anything either."

"But Grimshaw seems to think there was more work done on this somewhere." He looked at her. "Question is, does he just want the material? Or does he want to make sure nothing further was developed?"

"I'm not sure. Probably both."

"Is there anywhere else Nathan could have stashed more information?"

"That's what I came here to find out."

It only took a split second for him to follow. "The photo."

"Why else would he put it in there? It was the only thing other than the notes and the diskette in the box. I don't know. Maybe there was something on the diskette for me. Maybe I should have broken it."

John shook his head. "I don't think so. He didn't have time. Maybe he intended to leave something more substantial in there for you later on. But he also knew that the disk could be decrypted. A note to you on there would have been decrypted right along with it. But the photo—"

"Meant something only to me."

"Exactly."

"I know it's not much to go on. I didn't know what else to try. At first I thought they'd leave me alone once they were convinced I didn't have anything else. They didn't want my help, so I thought they'd taken it in-house to resolve. Instead they just took my house."

John tossed his pen down. "So all you have now is the photo? You want me to protect you from people who are trying to kill you for something you don't even have?"

"McShane, if they believed me, trust me, I wouldn't be here right now. But they don't. I've told them everything, they've taken the rest."

"They came after you after they cleaned you out?"

"Yes. I was followed. Two men tried to take me in the parking garage of my condo building. I managed to get loose and run. They shot at me."

"Why not call the police?"

"No, I wasn't hit. Thanks for asking." His lack of concern shouldn't have rankled, but it did. She crossed her arms. "They were less than helpful with my condo problem. I guess I didn't want to give them another chance to ridicule me about paranoia plots and mental instability."

"They are investigating, though."

"Yes, but I could be dead by the time they find a trail."

"So you hopped a plane to Martinique."

"What other choice did I have? I figured my only hope was to come here and try to find out something about what Nathan was working on."

"To turn over to Grimshaw?"

"Not hardly." Tiring of hashing out the whole

ordeal, knowing it was far from over, she leaned back in her chair and took a moment to pull herself together. "I don't know what to do, John. Frankly, I don't know who the good guys are anymore. They don't wear those convenient little white hats."

McShane leaned forward. His eyes darkened with what she could almost mistake for concern. Obviously she was more fatigued than she thought. His next words proved it.

"Here's my solution. Nathan's dead. The project, whatever it is, died with him. For all you know, the reason for not wanting it to go public or get in the wrong hands is political and nothing more. So make a deal. Tell them why you came to Martinique. Let them follow up on it. Tell them to leave you out of it from that point on, or you'll take the same story to the media. Then get out."

She pushed out of her chair, leaning right into his face. "Excuse me, but you can't really believe it's that simple. They've tried to shoot me! And what if you're wrong, McShane? Huh? What if I'm right and Nathan died for this? I don't know what the program does, or why they are willing to kill for it. But they were ten years ago, and they sure as hell are now. I'm not handing anything over to anyone until I know just what it is I'm giving to them."

"Cali, you don't have anything to hand—"

"Yet, McShane. Yet. I have a lead—"

"Are you sure the people shooting at you were connected to this?"

"What?" She'd kept a lid on her temper for so

long during the past weeks that it was packed inside her like a live grenade. John had just pulled the pin. "I'm sure I might have disappointed a client or two in my life, but none of them have taken a shot at me over it."

"In this business it pays not to overlook any possibility. No jilted lovers?"

She circled the table. He shoved his chair back. She pushed a finger into his chest as he rose. "No. No jilted lovers. It's connected. And I will not be responsible for reintroducing a potentially dangerous piece of technology to the world. If I'm right and Nathan did die over this, then I have his death to avenge and clear up too." Her chest was heaving at this point. She tried to take a breath. "If you don't want to help, fine, don't. It's not your battle. If you know of someone who will, I'd appreciate a name. But this time I'm doing it my way, McShane. And I'm not stopping until I'm satisfied that it's over once and for all."

John grabbed her arm as she swung away and pulled her back to face him. "Fine. Then let me take over. I'll find you a safe place until we get it all figured out."

He watched as her mouth opened, then shut again as his offer sank in. What in the hell had she thought he was going to do? Abandon her?

He swore silently. He had abandoned her once before.

She hadn't needed him then, he countered. He looked into eyes filled with pain and righteous anger. She needed him now.

He loosened his grip. "Let me help you, Cali."

She tugged her arm gently from his grasp but didn't step away. He could smell the scent of shampoo in her hair, could feel the heat of her skin.

"I won't be tucked away. I didn't call you in to take on the risk—"

"You do battle with microchips. I step in front of bullets for a living."

"I'm not asking you to be a human shield, McShane."

Her lack of gratitude shouldn't have stung.

"I was hoping you could use whatever contacts you still have to track this backward, try to find out who Grimshaw answers to, while I try to dig up whatever it was Nathan might have left here."

"I'm already here. I can put in a few calls and get that going and work on this end too. I still think you'd be better off underground for a while."

Temper flashed in her eyes. "Well, I'm sorry but I don't agree. We're playing this my way. I want your help but I won't be shoved aside."

He found himself lifting a piece of hair away from her damp cheek. She pulled back in surprise. He frowned and stepped away. He curled his hands into loose fists to keep from following his instincts. Instincts that all but screamed at him to pull her into his arms, to do whatever it took to keep her safe.

He did the next best thing.

"Does your father know you are bouncing around the world with hit men on your trail?"

"No. And he won't know anything about this, either." Her eyes narrowed. "You wouldn't dare."

"Cali, don't you think he should—"

"I think Ambassador Stanfield should be left alone to do his job. His daughter is a grown woman who can run her own life."

"That life is in jeopardy. Don't you think he has a right to know that?"

"You don't play fair, McShane." She blew out a sigh and pushed her hair off her forehead. She paced to the sink, then turned to face him again. "It took me a whole bunch of years to get out from under my father's rather oppressive protection. The way I met you and Nathan is as good an example as anything. You know firsthand what he's like when he wants something done."

John most certainly did. Cali had been snatched from a multinational dinner she'd been hostessing for her father in an increasingly unstable part of the Middle East. In fact, the dinner had been a kind of peace-seeking summit, in hopes of easing some of the tension. John remembered quite well the way Ambassador Stanfield, a former navy admiral, had bulled in and taken charge of the rescue effort. John and Nathan had led the Blue Circle recovery team.

They'd been shorthanded at the time, and John had pulled Nathan in from his usual "truck" position monitoring surveillance information. In the end it had been Nathan who'd gone in and rescued her from the hotel the terrorists had her stashed in, while John had reduced their number by a handful.

They hadn't even gotten her out of the country before she and Nathan had discovered their mutual obsession with advanced computer technology. Any doubts John held regarding love, the first-sight variety or any other, dissolved over the following months at the ongoing spectacle of the new couple's obvious feelings for each other.

Unfortunately, John's understanding was not the result of observation alone. It came from personal experience.

"It's also a good example that his concerns over your welfare were well-founded," John interjected.

"One incident in my entire life does not excuse his obsessive need to control." She continued when he would have interrupted. "I know, I know. It was a very bad situation. In that case, he had every right."

"You're all he has." Her mother's death from breast cancer when Cali was fifteen had been well documented by the media at the time. And John understood overprotective parents better than she knew. His father had been a high-ranking military officer when John had made his surprise entrance into the world late in the man's life. He understood Cali's need to be totally independent. For her it had been a means to escape her father's dominance, and later a way to overcome the helpless feelings spawned by her tragic losses.

"You don't know him like I do. He has always been as much a controller as a leader. His whole life was geared to suit his own needs. And he wasn't above using my mother's death to emotionally manipulate me into being a follower."

"It says a lot about your ability to be your own leader that you broke away and worked for the government. In high-security matters, no less."

"It was the hardest thing I'd ever done." He saw the slight shiver race over her skin. "I was terrified, but I knew I had to take a stand."

"My experience is that what you gain in personal growth, in strength, from standing up to what you fear most is something you can't put a price on."

"You're right," she said quietly. "Still," she went on, "I never made the mistake of thinking I was immune to his tactical emotional weapons. He didn't win all those war medals for nothing." Her attention shifted inwardly. "If I hadn't had Nathan—" She broke off and looked away.

John let her have the moment to collect herself, not at all sure what he would—or should—do anyway.

He hated indecision. His intellect was at war with his emotions—a common problem when dealing with Cali Ellis. He could almost sympathize with her father.

"My father trusted Nathan. It was the perfect compromise. I would marry a man I loved, one who'd already proven he could protect an ambassador's daughter. I was able to get out again, live like a normal person." Her voice faltered. "For six whole months."

"I'm sorry, Cali." And he was. As much as he'd

wanted her, still wanted her, he'd never wished her to be in pain.

"It was a tough time. With Nathan gone and my difficulty with my miscarriage, I knew my father would demand that I come back and stay with him as he had after the kidnapping. I couldn't, John. I know he loves me, but I just couldn't. I think that's partly why I called you that night."

She looked across the room at him, her expression almost begging him to understand. He had to force himself to stay put. "Cali—"

"No, let me say it. I knew that when push came to shove, you wouldn't make me do anything I didn't really want to do. I also knew you wouldn't let me wallow in my grief either. I'm sorry I put you in such a tough position—"

"Cali, stop." John closed the distance between them before he'd consciously decided to move. He stopped just in front of her. When she wouldn't look at him, he cupped her cheek. Once their eyes met he let his hand fall away.

"I shouldn't have left you when I did. I should have stayed. Helped you somehow."

"No, that's not true. I'd already asked more from you than I had a right to. He was your friend, too, and I wasn't letting you grieve the way you wanted to, needed to."

He traced the smooth line of her jaw, fully aware of the fine trembling sensation that radiated to his fingertips. "I'm not going to tell your father anything about this."

"Thank you."

"I'll help you, Cali. But we have to work as a team. You're going to have to trust me at some point."

"I'm trying. I do. Just don't ask me to step aside and let someone else fix my life. I can't do that. I won't do that."

A knock on the front door made them both jump.

Cali turned away first. "Coming."

John grabbed her arm and pulled her back. "Are you expecting anyone?"

"It's probably Eudora. She was supposed to come and get some flowers to take to a sick friend of hers in the village. She's owned this property for decades." She smiled. "I'd guess you'd say she's my landlady."

He knew Cali needed some relief from the tension. But if she really wanted to be in control of her life, she needed to understand right now what that entailed. "Humor me," he said.

He started toward the door, intending to peek into the front room, when Cali called out, "Who's there?"

"I came for the flowers," came a strong, heavily accented voice.

Cali shot him a smug look. "You've been playing super-secret spy for too long, McShane. No one knows I'm down here. I didn't tell anyone but you about the picture."

She slipped past him before he could react. He was on her heels as she entered the front room.

The strident, French-accented voice was at odds with the woman standing on the other side of the screen. Eudora was tiny, her skin weathered and dark, her gray hair, what was left of it, scraped tightly to her head in a thin twist. But even her stooped posture couldn't disguise the energy that fairly vibrated from her.

She held a large, shirt-sized box that she lifted slightly as Cali entered the empty front room.

"This came for you, *chérie*. In today's mail."

THREE

"Finally! I wondered when it would get here."

John snagged her arm before she could open the door. He tugged her back. "I thought you said no one knew you were here?" His fierce whisper was hot in her ear.

Cali frowned at him. "Hush, I'll explain later. I don't want Eudora in this. The woman doesn't miss a trick."

"She owned this place when you were here with Nathan. Surely you've questioned her."

"Yes," she all but hissed under breath. "But there are ways to do it that don't involve a single, bare lightbulb and bamboo shoots."

"I've never used bamboo shoots."

She stilled, then shot him an approving look. "I didn't think you were capable."

He lifted a brow. "Of torture?"

She smiled dryly. "Of humor. I know firsthand

about your ability to torture." She patted him on the arm. "You don't need anything as crude as bamboo."

She eased her arm from his grip and turned back to Eudora. The old woman's attention was focused intently on both of them. "I'm sorry, let me introduce you." Opening the door, she relieved her landlady of her burden. "Eudora, this is an old acquaintance, John McShane. John, this is Eudora Magdelane. She was kind enough to open this place back up for me."

Eudora squinted, adding wrinkles to a face Cali had thought already filled to capacity. Sharp black eyes scanned John from head to toe and back before she finally extended a hand.

Cali watched in amused silence as John stepped closer and took the gnarled, tanned fingers in his own much larger hand. Her mouth dropped open in shock when he smiled and lifted Eudora's hand to his mouth, dropping a polite kiss before tucking her hand in his.

"My pleasure, mademoiselle," he said smoothly.

Cali's gaze drifted from John to Eudora. She was beaming as if courted by a royal suitor. John McShane, charming? Cali shook her head. It must be the heat.

She turned and walked back to the kitchen. "I'll be right back with your flowers."

"Oh, take your time, *chérie*," the old woman trilled. Eudora never trilled. "I'm in no hurry."

"I'll bet you aren't," Cali muttered. She sat the package on the table, wondering how rude it would be just to open it now. Not that they'd notice, she thought, listening to Eudora's uncharacteristic chatter and John's attentive responses. But the contents were too important to risk being seen by anyone but her or John.

She was surprised Eudora had taken it upon herself to deliver the package. Probably hoping to discover what was inside, Cali thought. The old snoop.

She slid the poinsettias from the vase and carefully wrapped the stems in a wet towel, then plastic bagged them, before returning to the front room. Eudora and John were still standing just inside the door.

Cali had been on Martinique for almost two weeks. In that time she'd engaged Eudora in conversation any number of times. If you could call their brief exchanges that. She'd discovered Eudora could rival the sneakiest interrogator when she wanted to know something, but was notoriously closemouthed when the tables were turned.

When Cali had first arrived, she'd been relieved to find the cottage still standing, though obviously unoccupied for some time. Ten years earlier, Nathan had rented the cottage from Eudora's son, Adrian. But at some point during the interim, he had left the property in his mother's inimitable care. Eudora was every bit as shrewd as her son. Cali had thought to play on the woman's sympathies by concocting a sad story about revisiting the site of her honeymoon ten years after the death of her poor young husband. She knew Nathan would have forgiven her the subterfuge. But when Eudora had taken Cali's request under consideration like a woman with a waiting list of dozens,

Cali had changed tactics, appealing to the woman's more mercenary side.

Eudora was typical of some of the French-descended population on the island in that she was cordial and hospitable, but only to a point. As had been Cali's experience a decade before, those particular inhabitants operated with the understanding that while tourism played an important role in their economy, they didn't have to like it. Especially when said tourists were Americans. She'd felt more tolerated than welcomed.

Cali had spent long, frustrating, mostly unsuccessful hours trying to pry information out of the woman. Time she didn't have. But Eudora was not a woman to be rushed.

"Here you go," she said, holding the cut plants out.

The woman was beaming up at John. Not rushed perhaps, Cali thought, but courted . . . Well, that was one angle that had been unavailable to her. Until now.

Without meeting her eyes, John smoothly relieved her of the heavy bouquet then turned back to Eudora. Cali reined in the urge to kick him. She knew he was trying to help. But who knew the man could smile convincingly, much less be charming? Where had all that charm been when she'd been bleeding to death and had needed soft words?

All she'd gotten was ill-tempered orders to stop whining and get off her duff and get back to her life.

She ignored the fact that his tactics had worked, where her doctor's gentle care had not.

"Quite an exotic bouquet." John laid the flowers gently in Eudora's waiting arms. "Your garden is—"

"A mess," Eudora finished bluntly. She turned, finally acknowledging Cali's presence. "Cali here is slowly taming it. My son . . ." She purposely drifted off, lifting her shoulders in that world-weary way Cali imagined Gallic women had perfected centuries ago. "He lives all his life here, then three months ago—*poof!* He tells me his destiny is not on the island of his birth, where centuries of Magdelanes have resided, but in America." She all but spat the last word, all the while holding their gazes with an arrogance that didn't give the least indication she thought she might have offended them.

Cali stilled. She'd wondered about Adrian, but the old woman had been characteristically silent on that subject. She turned to John, counting on him to charm more information out of his latest suspect.

She frowned. John's congenial smile was gone, replaced by the alert expression with which Cali was all too familiar.

"Where did he move to?" he asked without preamble.

Eudora's dark eyes narrowed, her expression grew distant. "What is the difference?" She favored John with a brief once-over, her small sniff making it clear he was no longer in her favor. "Gone is gone." She turned to Cali. "These will do, *chérie*. You will have the bird of paradise ready for tomorrow, no?"

Cali stifled a sigh of disappointment and pulled out a smile. "No later than early afternoon, if that's okay."

The woman nodded and stepped to the door. She paused briefly. She didn't have to look at John to make her expectations understood.

John felt Cali's stare drilling him in the back. But he knew better than to push the old woman. He'd blown it big time. But he could grill Eudora on her absent son another time. Right now he wanted to know what was in that box. He opened the screen. "A pleasure to meet you," he said, not expecting a response. He wasn't disappointed.

"Thank you for delivering the package," Cali called out from just behind his shoulder. Eudora merely lifted her flower-laden arms in response and continued to trudge along the cobblestone path that led back to the nearby village of Aleria.

"Quite a character," John commented.

He turned in time to catch Cali's somewhat smug smile. "She's a nosy old busybody with too much on the ball and just enough savvy to be dangerous with it." She led the way to the kitchen. "She was rather taken with you, though. So obviously senility is finally creeping in."

"Hey," he protested. "What did I do to deserve that?" He followed her into the kitchen. "If she's been here all this time, she might know something that would help. And it might be coincidence, but her son disappearing just about the time your troubles began is worth looking into."

Cali sighed in exasperation. "Give me some credit, McShane. I've spent hours with the woman, none of them remotely relaxed. She could write manuals on interrogation techniques. I spent more time trying to make sure I wouldn't give anything away than finagling any worthwhile information out of her." She smiled. "You were going gangbusters there for a while. A sense of humor *and* charm. Who'd have thought it? What other attributes have you hidden from me?"

"I have nothing to hide." That particular lie tasted quite bitter. But there were some truths that should never be revealed. "And I've been told on more than one occasion that I can be quite charming."

"So it's just me who is favored with this side of your lovely personality. Thanks." She beat him to the counter and the package. She carried it to the table.

He nodded to the box. "You ask me to give you credit, yet you do something as foolish as give someone—anyone—your forwarding address. Why didn't you just leave a trail of bread crumbs?" He jerked his thumb toward the front door. "There won't be a soul within fifteen miles of here who won't know you got a package today."

"It never occurred to me she'd deliver it. In fact, I'd have bet money she'd be the last one to do it."

"Why did she, then?"

"Curiosity. The woman is an incurable gossip. About everyone except herself, that is."

"That could be useful to us, too, if she knows

enough people. Played right, she could be a valuable source without her knowing it."

"Well, don't look at me. I tried. You're the one with the killer smile and Casanova charm. Of course, you may have to butter her up all over again. I can't believe a seasoned veteran like you blew it so badly. I also can't believe I just described you as charming either. For all I know, that was a fluke and this"—she gestured at his frowning, stiff countenance—"is the real you after all."

"You're stalling again, Cali."

"And you're digressing again, McShane." But she conceded the point and took a knife from the table, using it to slit open the brown tape sealing the box.

John placed a hand on her wrist, stopping her. "Not so fast. You said you were expecting this. How do you know it hasn't been tampered with? Who did you trust, Cali? Who else knows you're here?"

"Off-island? Only two people. You and the safety-deposit-box officer from the bank on Grand Cayman." She shook his hand free and finished opening the box. "He's overseen Nathan's box the entire time."

John gripped her arm again. She sighed in exasperation, but stopped. "What?"

"Well, the setup that Nathan had with the bank is highly unusual."

"Yes, but you forget, he worked for some pretty unusual people over the years. Who knows what sort of contacts he had. As for the bank officer, it's not odd for someone to keep the same job for many years."

She slanted him a look. "You're still a super-spy, you can relate."

John wondered if she'd kept track of him. He'd taken Seve Delgado's offer to be part of his highly specialized team shortly after Nathan's death. The basic tenet of the Dirty Dozen squad's philosophy was "All for one and only one." Meaning, duty came first and there was no second. It had been the perfect choice of job for a man who had spent his whole life making sure his only duty was to himself.

The original dozen had been handpicked for a wide variety of reasons. But the one thing they all had in common was that, outside of the team, they had absolutely no ties to anyone. Not family, not friends. No one.

They were inviolable. No ties meant no weaknesses, no vulnerable spots that could be exploited by their enemies, the trump card used most often in his line of work.

But even the team members were human. Half the squad had been lost during various missions, but the other losses had occurred when several agents had fallen prey to the human need for the one thing they weren't allowed to have. Ties.

Delgado himself had almost lost an important case and his own life to protect a daughter no one had known he had. The team member sent in to protect her had lost his heart.

John looked down at his hand. Cali's pulse thrummed beneath his thumb. Links. Ties.

He was tied to this woman in ways he couldn't

begin to fathom. This was the last place on earth he should be—and the only place he wanted to be.

He pulled his hand away. "So, this was sent by the bank? I thought you'd collected it all. Notes and a photo."

"I was trying to get to that, but Eudora interrupted us before I could. I don't know for sure if what's in here is connected or not."

"Where did it come from?"

"Apparently, Nathan opened more than one safety-deposit box. I stopped in Grand Cayman to officially close the account and the box, only to find out he had two of them."

"And you're just now telling me?" He swallowed the urge to shout. Jaw tight, he asked, "Couldn't you tell from the statements that there was an unaccounted-for payment?"

"At the time I didn't pay close attention and just assumed the payments were for the one box he had. Since my name wasn't on this box, I had to wrangle with the bank to get them to open it. They demanded all sorts of documents proving I was Nathan's sole heir. Which, since my condo was ripped off, wasn't easy. I got it all faxed in, but there was a waiting period while they approved it. I didn't want to wait any longer to get here and start digging."

"Then they notified you here?"

"Of course not. I told them I'd check back with them."

"Then why did you have them send the stuff

rather than pick it up yourself? That's a direct link."
John didn't want to think about links.

She looked away, busying herself with pulling out the packing paper then lifting out a fat manila envelope.

"Bank officers, even those working for highly confidential banks like the ones on Grand Cayman, can still be gotten to, Cali."

She rooted through the rest of the packing papers, but found nothing else. She finally looked at him again.

"Maybe I was hoping you'd really come," she said quietly. "I didn't want to risk being gone if you came."

John tried to ignore the shadow of vulnerability he found in her eyes. "Then you should have waited until after I arrived to pick it up."

The shadow disappeared. "I had no idea how long that might be. It's not as if I'm not aware of what is involved here, McShane. I've worked on numerous top-secret assignments."

"That was ten years ago. You said yourself you've only done civilian work since Nathan's death."

"Time doesn't change the basic rules for protecting yourself. I'm not naive." She paused for a moment, as if waiting for him to refute the statement. After several seconds of silence, her shoulders dipped, losing some of their rigidity.

"But," she added, "I have to be honest. Though I am absolutely sure I didn't leave a trail, I admit that I wasn't comfortable about letting any more time pass without doing everything I could. I was Nathan's wife and acknowledged heir to his other accounts with the bank, yet they still put me through the wringer before letting me have access to the second safety-deposit box. Given that, I felt as secure as I could that they wouldn't reveal any information to anyone else regarding my business there. That is why people bank there in the first place."

"Nothing is foolproof, Cali. You shouldn't have left any connection to Martinique. And you better than anyone know that if human weakness can't be exploited, there is always someone who can exploit a technological one."

"I doubt anyone hacked their way into the bank's computer. And even so, that would show account activity, but not forwarding addresses."

"I wouldn't be so sure."

"Well, it's a moot point because I had it mailed to Aleria under a different name." She flipped the box flap and pointed to the label on the box. "MWJ, Inc. It's phony. It's my mom's maiden initials. I opened a post office box here and I've checked it every day. The return address is also a phony. It's an off-island secured holding facility the bank uses for unclaimed property. I guess someone could trace that if they worked hard enough, but really, I don't—"

"How did Eudora know this was yours, then?"

His quietly spoken question cut through the steamy afternoon air like a sharp gust of cold air. Even Cali's sun-flushed cheeks paled.

"Oh my God," she whispered. "I didn't even

think—I mean, you had just shown up and I was so surprised and so relieved. And then Eudora was there with the box and it didn't occur to me to that she shouldn't know—"

"By accepting the package, you acknowledged you are MWJ, Inc."

Her eyes widened. "You don't think this means *she's* in on the whole mess somehow, do you?"

John's expression betrayed none of the turmoil going on inside his head. He had a very bad feeling about all of this. "In your talks with her, did you ever mention that you were waiting for a package?"

She shook her head. "I'm certain of that. I stuck to my story that I was here on a sort of sentimental journey on the tenth anniversary of my husband's death. She'd probably have heard I got mail after the fact, but what difference would that have made?" She looked down at the envelope and then toward the door Eudora had left through. "I guess there's no point in going after her now."

"It won't do us any good anyway." John turned and paced to the counter and back, raking his hand through his damp hair. "Whatever she might know she won't give up to us." He turned back to face her.

She began to peel open the sealed flap. She glanced up at him, her eyes filled with both excitement and a healthy dose of trepidation.

John crossed the room and slid the opened package from her hands. She grabbed for them, but he was too fast.

"Hey!"

"I don't know where the hell my head is." He knew exactly where it was. On Cali instead of on the job. "I shouldn't have let you open the box without me checking it first. That Eudora knew it was for you alerted me, but I thought you'd slipped and given out your address. Dammit, Cali, this whole thing could have been rigged."

Understanding dawned on her face. "Makes sense. Why else deliver it to me in the first place? If Eudora is somehow working for the black hats, she'd have just taken the box and delivered it to her boss. I'd never have known it arrived. But she did deliver it, so that either means . . ."

He studied the thick envelope. "That it's a trap of some kind. That someone on the island suspected you're MWJ, Incorporated and passed that information on innocently to Eudora or—"

"No, she'd have said something. She wouldn't let something unusual like that pass without a question." She stared pointedly at John. "Of course, she *was* a bit distracted."

John didn't react. He'd just been doing his job. Something he managed to do easily with everyone on the planet but Cali Ellis. Ellis. She'd signed her note that way. Meaning she hadn't remarried. He found his gaze straying to her ring finger and purposely pulled it back in, forcing his mind back to the matter at hand.

"Then there is the curious coincidence of her son leaving the island just when this whole fiasco began. We don't rule her out."

"Okay, then," she said. "Why deliver it to me? Why not keep it?"

"For all we know they've been through it already."

"The men who are after me are here?"

John shook his head. "My instincts say no. They might have traced your faxes to Cayman and intercepted the package before it left."

"If that's true, that still doesn't explain Eudora or why it was sent on to me."

"They could pass it on to you, then follow you. I'm not sure about Eudora's role at this point."

Cali shivered despite the hotter-than-average weather. She rubbed the sudden gooseflesh on her arms. "This is almost too paranoid even for me to believe."

"Don't be stupid, Cali. We're talking about people who made the contents of your condo disappear in the space of a day. Whatever Nathan was into must have been mighty powerful for them to launch a campaign like this. Rule number one: Never underestimate your opponent." He held her gaze until she lowered her hands and squared her shoulders.

"I was only trying to do the right thing, John. I didn't ask for this. Any of it. But I can't just hand over whatever is in that envelope or whatever information it might lead us to uncover without first figuring out just what it is I have stumbled into."

"Even at the risk of your life?"

She paled again, but her eyes flashed. The contrast made him want to yank her behind him, to protect her from risking herself and doing anything foolish. And at the same time he wanted to pull her into his arms, soothe her fears, promise her he'd fight this battle for her if she'd just promise to keep herself safe in return.

He could do neither. Nor could he extract that sort of promise from her. She wouldn't give it. And he couldn't allow her, or anyone, to matter that much to him.

Or rather, he could never let anyone know how much she already mattered. Least of all Cali herself.

"I don't see where I really have a choice on risk, McShane. The bullets are already flying."

He'd liked it better when she called him John. "You could let me put you somewhere safe while I figure this out."

"No way. We already covered this ground. This is my fight. Whoever it is was responsible for Nathan's death. I feel it in my bones. And if that's not enough, now they've come after me too." She crossed the room and snatched the envelope from his hands, turned, and emptied the contents onto the table. A three-ring binder stuffed thick with well-worn paper fell out.

But it was the stack of diskettes that drew their undivided attention. Cali pinned him with her gaze. "Will you help me find Nathan's killers, John?"

FOUR

Say yes.

Cali repeated the words silently over and over as she stared him down. She had no idea what he was thinking. She hoped McShane couldn't see how badly she was shaking inside. Bullets really were flying. She meant every word she'd said, but that didn't mean she wasn't scared out of her mind.

"Well," she said with far more bravery than she felt. "What's it going to be?"

He was silent for several more nerve-stretching seconds, then finally shifted his gaze back to the diskettes. "These are five-and-a-quarter floppies. We'll have to find an older CPU."

It wasn't exactly an enthusiastic avowal of support, but it was all she could do not to slump forward in abject relief. She desperately wanted to take five and regroup. She'd barely adapted to island time, and now things were popping too fast. But she didn't have that luxury.

"Did you bring a PC with you?" he asked.

"I had an entire room filled with state-of-the-art equipment and enough software to make even Bill Gates drool." She snapped her fingers. "All gone."

He glanced at her. "I take it that's a no."

Cali fought an unexpected smile. Watching John flirt with Eudora had bothered her in ways it shouldn't have. But now, with his newly revealed charm directed at her, she wondered if she'd been too hasty with her silent wishes.

He was intimidating enough. A charming John McShane was the last thing she wanted. Correction, her mind intruded. A charming John McShane was the last thing she needed. *But be honest, Cali. You want it. You want him.*

John McShane? She shoved the whole absurd idea out of her mind. "That would be a no."

He sighed in obvious exasperation. The McShane she knew—irascible, impatient, and never satisfied—returned. She relaxed a notch. This was familiar territory.

"How did you expect to analyze whatever it is you found down here?" he demanded.

"With ancient hieroglyphics," she shot back. "Come on, I had no idea what, if anything, I would find. I more or less fled the country. I didn't have a master plan here, McShane."

"That's obvious."

His criticism stung more than it should have.

"Come on, it's not as if I went to super-spy school like some of us in this room. You have to admit I've done pretty well, all things considered." She broke off. The last thing she would ever do was seek his approval. She'd lost that battle with him before, during the lowest time of her life. A time when one kind word from him would have meant everything.

She lifted the binder. "Let's start with this. Maybe it will tell us what is on the diskettes. Then we'll worry about tracking down a PC." She pulled out a chair and sat down.

She flipped open the cover, but John was still standing on the other side of the table. She could feel his attention focused on her. It wasn't unpleasant.

She looked up, and her heart jumped. Maybe it was the heat. It most definitely could have been the stress. But for a split second, she could have sworn she'd seen— No. No, she was mistaken. There was no way John McShane would ever look at her with what might—in a man who had feelings—be mistaken for tenderness.

The very idea that he could feel such an emotion at all shook her up more than she cared to admit. Because if she cared to admit it, which until an hour ago she'd have sworn she didn't, the idea of an emotional John McShane, whether it be charm or tenderness, was fast becoming an all-too-appealing proposition.

"John?" His name came out much too huskily. She cleared her throat.

His expression was fathomless once again. Yet as

the silence grew and he continued to look at her, Cali felt a very specific heat begin to curl inside of her. It had been quite some time since she'd felt that particular warmth, but she knew exactly what it was—*want*.

Want, which was not to be confused with need. There was no doubt she needed John McShane. Her very life probably depended on him.

But want . . . That was another thing entirely.

She'd lost too much. In the last ten years she'd allowed herself to want very few things, even less when it came to men. The risk of combining need with want was one she couldn't take. Not yet. Maybe never again. Certainly not with John McShane.

The scraping of chair legs broke her thoughts. Feeling her cheeks heat, somehow knowing he wouldn't miss the telltale sign, she turned her attention back to the binder.

She stilled for a split second when, instead of sitting in the chair, he dragged it around the table to a spot right next to her elbow. She'd never felt the heat of close proximity quite this way. She gathered the loose blank pages and fitted them back on the rings, then flipped quickly past the next few blank pages.

He turned the chair and straddled it, then reached for the diskettes. There were four of them. She watched as he slid each one from its protective sleeve and examined both sides.

"No labels?" she said.

He shook his head and dropped the stack on the empty envelope. He turned to her. "Let's see what you've got."

His eyes were so clear. She didn't remember that quality, but she did remember the coldness.

They weren't cold now.

She cleared her suddenly tight throat and looked back at the binder. "Nothing but blank pages so far." She flipped past another half dozen. "Why would he have gone to the trouble to set up a safety-deposit box just to keep an empty notebook in it?" She glanced at John. "Makes me wonder if the disks are blank too." She shook her head and thumbed slowly through another couple of pages, careful not to tear them from the metal rings.

Suddenly John slid the notebook from her. "Wait a minute."

Cali's mouth dropped open in protest. He wasn't paying any attention to her. "I was trying not to tear anything. They're blank, but the edges are worn, as if he's been through this binder a hundred times."

"Exactly," John said, positioning the book in front of him. He slid his fingers about halfway into the book and carefully flipped the pages over. "Still blank."

She frowned. "Well, other than invisible ink, I don't—"

"You wouldn't happen to have an ultraviolet light around, would you?"

"I was kidding about invisible ink." She paused, but when he didn't respond, she added, "But you're not, are you?"

"Is there a greenhouse around here somewhere?"

"The whole island is one giant greenhouse. Even I

could grow things here. But no," she added when he sighed with impatience, "I don't think there is a commercial one close by." She looked at the supposed empty pages again, tilting her head and squinting. "Is there any other way to determine if there really is something on this page?"

"Not without ruining the paper in the process."

"Why would he do this? Even ten years ago, the bad guys could figure out how to use ultraviolet light."

"But would anyone have given a blank book a second glance?"

"One put in a safety-deposit box? It's likely we aren't the only ones who would figure it out."

"More than likely he did it as a safety measure while he was actively working on the journal. I doubt he intended to stash it away at the time. And once he did, there was certainly no reason to alter its form."

Cali snapped her fingers. "You know anything about processing film?"

"What's your angle?"

"I was thinking about the red light they use in a darkroom."

"That's just a safelight to keep the film from overprocessing while it's developed."

"I know, but what about the chemicals used to develop the film? I took photography eons ago in high school. I don't remember all the technical stuff, but I do know the basic principle. Prints are made on light-sensitive paper."

"You think the chemicals used in the process might bring up the print?"

"Would that work?"

Something that might have been respect lurked in his expression. She didn't look too closely. It was easier to pretend she was right than chance being proven wrong.

"That might do it. It's a place to start." He glanced around. "If we're right, then whatever is on this paper is ten years old. It could ruin the notes altogether."

"We have to try. We'll only have to lose one page to find out. There is a photo shop in the village." She smiled dryly. "Their one concession to tourism, and a reluctant one at that."

"Charming place."

"Paradise can be hell."

His mouth softened into a brief smile. "I don't suppose they'd let us borrow the darkroom for a couple of hours."

"I would imagine that will depend on how much money you're willing to spend. They're bigger on renting than lending around here."

"Ah yes, the heart of a generous host, but the soul of a slumlord."

"Why should paradise be any different than the rest of the world?"

"You've grown cynical, Cali."

She eyed him. "Yeah, well, some of us are just slower on the uptake."

He didn't say anything, and she thought she saw

the respect in his expression change to disappointment. Her already-strung-too-tight nerves twanged a little. "I'm sorry, did you think you'd cornered that market? Or is cynicism permitted only to jaded, world-weary super-spies?"

"Will you cut it out with the super-spy thing?" He shoved a hand through his hair, looking peeved.

Another emotion surfaces. McShane, sensitive? She'd thought him impervious to the opinion of others. But like it or not, his sensitivity to the subject caught at her. As did everything about him.

She scowled. "Only if you cut it out with the 'let's rescue the poor blonde from herself' attitude."

"I never said anything like that."

"With you, words generally aren't necessary." His frown deepened. She lifted a hand before he could respond. "Truce. I'm sorry. Really. It's tension and stress on my part. No excuse, I know, since I asked you to join this little party."

He folded his arms on the back of the chair and regarded her silently. She wasn't aware she was grinding her teeth until her jaw began to ache. "It's just that, as you know, I have a little trouble with authority types." His sudden smile did next to nothing to slow the rollercoaster of her emotions. How could she be angry and incredibly turned on at the same time?

"You sit there and stare at me with that damned inscrutable 'I know more about life than you could ever hope to, girly-girl' look, and it drives me insane."

He lifted one eyebrow. "Girly-girl? I don't believe I would ever say that, nor would I ever mean to insinuate it." He straightened his back and his arms at the same time.

It was not a great time to notice the wire-hard veins under his tan skin or how sculpted his forearms were.

"As to you having blond moments . . ." He shrugged.

She smacked him hard on the shoulder. He didn't so much as flinch, but she could tell she'd surprised him.

They both stared at each other. John cracked first. His chuckle modulated into an honest-to-goodness laugh. It was rich and deep-timbred. It totally transformed him.

His eyes held warmth when he laughed. The lines fanning out from the corners, which normally underscored his "been there done it all" adventurer look, now made him appear like a man who embraced life. She almost believed he laughed easily and often.

It hit her then just how little she truly knew about the man. Maybe he laughed all the time. Maybe he was the type who partied his way through assignments, never taking his life—or anyone else's—too seriously.

No. She hadn't gotten to know him very well by the time Nathan died, but the brief time they had shared had been intense. He'd been overly serious and overtly dedicated—as well as impatient, demanding, and intimidating. Especially when things—namely people—got in the way of his getting the job done.

She'd been one of those people.

As their laughter faded she watched the life and warmth slowly ebb out of his eyes.

"Why do you do that?" The question was out before she had a chance to think about the wisdom of asking it.

"What? Laugh?"

She knew he'd purposely misunderstood her. What was he hiding? What other emotions lurked under that cool, gray surface?

He shrugged, but for the first time Cali wondered at his apparent nonchalance. *What gets to you, John McShane?*

She leaned on one elbow, studying his face openly now. "You don't usually laugh, do you?"

If it was possible, his expression became even more remote. "I think we have better things to talk about than my sense of humor."

"I wasn't questioning that." She didn't know why she persisted, except that she'd discovered a nick in his armor. It beguiled her and distracted her. The combination was downright irresistible.

"There's a difference between comprehending that something is funny and allowing yourself to let go and laugh out loud. But my original question wasn't about you laughing. I just wondered why you shut down as soon as you realize you might actually be experiencing a positive, non-job-related emotion?" She realized immediately she'd gone too far. "Of course you seem to have no problem cutting loose with the more negative ones," she added dryly, hoping to ease the sudden tension.

He propped his elbow on the chair, mimicking her pose.

"Gee, I don't know, Doc," he said with mock sincerity. "But whatever I do, or don't do, works just fine for me. And if you want me to work for you, then let's can this psychoanalysis and concentrate on getting your butt out of a very tight sling, okay?"

She'd hit way too close to home. That only goaded her on. "Will you answer one question for me?" His scowl didn't intimidate her in the least. All of a sudden John McShane was very human to her. She was very attracted to that, despite common sense telling her she was crazy. "Then I promise we'll get back to unslinging my butt."

He actually groaned and slumped over, forehead pressed to his arm. It was so theatrical and uncharacteristic, it made her laugh.

He was silent for several moments, then she heard a gruff muffled, "What?"

"Why did you really come down here?"

There was a long pause, and she thought he wasn't going to answer. Then he lifted his head and looked right at her. "You needed me."

This time she couldn't detect the hint of a false note to his sincerity. Her insides twisted just a little. She also wondered what it would be like to be needed *by* him. The twinge tightened another little knot. It was disconcerting, but not in the least unpleasurable.

"Do you always go where you're needed?"

"It's my job."

"So, I'm just another assignment?" The idea

shouldn't have hurt. But it did. "What will this cost me?"

"The cost is no more questions." He sat up abruptly and shoved back from the table, snagging the binder as he stood. He walked from the room without another word.

Perplexed with his sudden departure, she stood and started after him. Halfway to the door she turned back. Scooping up the diskettes, she slid them in the envelope, then grabbed her backpack from the hook by the back door and slid the whole thing inside. John was waiting at the front door.

"Are we off to see the photo wizard?" Her attempt to ease the tension fell flat. He said nothing. He just stood there holding the door open. She sighed in defeat and walked out into the steamy afternoon heat. "You are a very hard man to get to know, John McShane," she said. "I don't know why I even tried."

He stepped onto the porch behind her.

When she didn't hear the shells crunch under his feet, she looked back over her shoulder. He was standing beneath a swath of blossom-heavy bougainvillea.

"Well?" She gestured to the path stretching between them. "It's not made of yellow bricks, but if we follow it, we will be in Aleria in less than ten minutes."

"I have no idea why I'm here." His quiet words seemed to flow through the muggy air.

She faced him fully. "You don't have to stay."

"Oh yes, I do. You may drive me crazy but you can't drive me away." He stepped off the porch and walked to her. "But you're not just another assignment, Cali Ellis."

John had no idea what in the hell had possessed him to make such a declaration. Cali would have let it drop. For all her directness and tenacity, she was also good at masking tension with humor, babbling on about anything.

He'd been surprised that she'd pushed things back there in the kitchen. It had occurred to him at that moment that he didn't really know her.

He didn't like that realization.

The only time he'd spent with her, she'd been at her worst, her most vulnerable. Otherwise he'd always seen her with Nathan, as half of a happy couple. He'd known her as wife and widow. He'd admired and respected both.

But who was Cali Ellis, woman? Independent Cali Ellis? Free Cali Ellis? Ten-years-older-and-wiser Cali Ellis?

Right now she was hunted Cali Ellis, he reminded himself harshly. Dragging his mind away from tantalizing thoughts he had no business tormenting himself with, he brushed past her.

Cali reached out and grabbed his arm, catching him by surprise and turning him easily back to her. She didn't let him go. "If I'm not just another assignment, then what am I?"

He felt each individual finger pressing into his arm. He was close enough to smell the heat on her skin. To see the fine blond hair, damp and darker than the rest, clinging to her cheek and forehead. He was close enough to see in her eyes whatever she chose to show him.

"What, McShane? Obligation? Old debt?"

He didn't look, didn't dare. Her words drew his attention to her mouth instead. He found no sanctuary there. Never in his life had he wanted to know what a woman's mouth tasted like as badly as he did Cali Ellis's.

At that exact moment he had no idea how he'd last another second without finding out.

"Pity case? Paid vacation?" She bludgeoned him, making him watch her too soft lips form harsh indictments. He heard anger and pain, which doubled the wound he felt when in reality he would give anything to take her mouth under his and kiss her until they both heard only the sounds of pleasure and need. He wanted to make the pain and anger go away. Both Cali's and his.

She stopped, her mouth parted slightly as she drew in a deep breath. Maybe he'd chosen the harder path after all.

He lifted his gaze and met hers head-on. Apparently hell came in many shapes and colors. Right now hell was slightly rounded and blazing green.

"Just say it, John. Whatever it is that caused you to answer a plea from a minor, decade-old, out-of-touch acquaintance."

"Does it matter so much, Cali?" He was drowning in an indignant green sea, and the only life preserver in sight was the very thing pulling him under. "You needed help. You asked me. Isn't it enough to know you'll get it?"

She didn't shift so much as a hair. Her spine was still rigid, her expression still focused intensely and exclusively on him. "It should be." Her fingers relaxed slightly, then she abruptly dropped his arm and looked away. "It should be," she said, her voice so low and soft, it barely reached him.

It reached someplace deep and dark inside him, where the light never penetrated, where his soul had resided in cool, undisturbed peace.

Until now. Until Cali.

Without questioning the intelligence of the action, already knowing the answer and completely unwilling to heed it, he reached out and touched her chin.

Her skin was warm and damp from the humidity. His fingertip glided over her skin as he traced upward to her mouth. He saw her lower lip quiver slightly and he tensed his fingers to pull away. But, as if sensing his intent, she looked up.

He slid his fingers along her jawbone, beginning a journey that held far greater risk than merely touching her.

The palms of his hands grazed her ears as he plunged his fingers into her hair, pulling her closer.

"Yes, it should be." His voice was rough. "But it isn't, is it, Cali?" He stepped closer to her, felt her knees brush his. His body was already rock-hard. He tilted her head back, staring deeply into her eyes. "Is it?" he demanded.

He wasn't sure what he'd hoped to find there. A reason to stop. An excuse to continue. He found neither. She simply returned his gaze, probing his eyes as he did hers. For the first time he wondered what she found. He knew in that moment that whatever it was, it wasn't nearly enough, would never be enough.

He dropped his hands and stepped away. Unprepared for his sudden release, Cali stumbled back a step. John automatically reached out to still her, but she shrugged him off.

"I'm sorry, Cali."

"Don't you dare." She advanced on him.

He stood his ground, which was feeling shakier by the second. "Things are difficult enough. You don't need me to—"

"What do you know about my needs, John McShane?"

"I was out of line—"

"Was I the one pushing you away?" She was almost nose to nose with him. "And since when has crossing the line bothered you? It sure as hell didn't stop you from bullying me ten years ago."

"I know. That's why I left."

His quiet words instantly deflated her. "What?"

"Pushing past the line is what I do, Cali. But, with you, my actions weren't always motivated by your best interest. I told myself I was just doing what was necessary to get you on your feet the only way I knew how."

"And you did. I hated you for it at the time, but you did." She lifted her hand.

He braced himself for her touch, not at all sure he could handle direct contact at that moment and still control his reaction.

He didn't think he'd moved so much as a hair, but she must have sensed his withdrawal. She let her hand drop back to her side. He thought he detected the slightest hint of hurt in her eyes. Remembering how he'd felt when she'd pulled away, he identified strongly with her feeling.

"I wasn't just doing it for your own good," he said. "I was saving myself as well."

"You were hurting too. I understand."

She understood nothing. He knew he should let it go, let her misunderstand, wade on out of this emotional pool and get back to the real business at hand.

But this is the real business, isn't it? his inner voice said. Getting Cali in your life again, once and for all exploring the possibilities.

He thought about the assignment he'd left to come there, the people who were counting on him. He mentally recited the bottom-line rule for any Dirty Dozen member and the only one he never broke. *No attachments of any kind.* Ignoring that rule had robbed the team of several members, including their former leader.

Commitment to anyone created a vulnerability that could be exploited. It wouldn't happen to him.

He'd dedicated himself to the Dirty Dozen ten years before. With Del gone and most of the team disbanded, they needed him now more than ever.

So did Cali, his little voice offered. Ultimately, he was expendable to the team—but *not to her*.

Which was precisely why he was there. The very idea of her needing him more than anyone else in the world was enough to keep him from walking away.

Saving her now, as he had a decade earlier, was all he could do for her. A rescuer was the only role he could play. Yes, they were both adults. He wasn't blind, he knew Cali was interested. He could push that line, have at least part of what he wanted so badly. He could tell himself that anything they shared was better than nothing.

He looked at her. His body remained hard, but his heart was getting softer by the second. He knew then that there would be no pushing any boundaries, no breaking of rules, because only one of them would be able to walk away unscathed.

And it wouldn't be him.

FIVE

Cali's emotions were a jumble of contradictions. She was feeling things for John she'd never expected to feel, and it was not the time to explore them. He was apparently grappling with some disconcerting feelings himself.

"We'd, uh, better get into town. It's getting late and most of the shops close up tight by five."

He was silent for a moment, then nodded. "Yeah, you're right. Let's go."

She was beginning to read him better. He was relieved she was letting what happened—or almost happened—drop. You'd never know by looking at him, far from it. But he'd given in.

It made her feel good to be able to understand him, as if she were a member of an exclusive club. Was there anyone in his life who had full access to the inner workings of his mind? To his thoughts and emotions? Had he ever given someone access to his heart? To his soul?

She walked faster down the gravel path, freely admitting to herself that she was running away both literally and figuratively.

If any woman had penetrated the walls he'd built to shield his personal life, she'd more than likely had to use a battering ram. That was assuming he even had a personal life.

Less than ten minutes later the path wandered out of the bordering banana plantations and into Aleria. The buildings were made mostly of whitewashed stone. Cali imagined that the overall look of the place hadn't changed much over the decades. Less than a dozen little businesses lined the one and only paved road. Of them, all but two were currently operational, offering a variety of services, including a small grocer, a Laundromat, a curio shop, a patisserie, and a small drugstore.

"There." She pointed to the small, mostly white building at the opposite end of the street.

"A *pharmacie*." Those had been the first words he'd uttered since they'd left the bungalow. "What is the owner's name again?"

"Monsieur Quéval. He runs the whole store, but photography is an interest of his. Eudora says he only opened his photo lab to the public as a way of financing his hobby."

"Eudora actually shared that tidbit with you? Downright chatty of her."

"Shrewd woman. She had to give something if she expected me to tell her anything."

"I'm glad she chose this."

Cali's smile was smug. "Yes. I'm sure she thought it was harmless information."

John pushed open the door to the dimly lit store. He let her pass, then ducked under the low, uneven door frame. Small bells tied to the back of the door announced their entrance. Inside, it smelled damp but felt refreshingly cool. The window air-conditioning unit was loud and wheezy, but it did the job. Cali blotted her forehead and cheeks on her T-shirt sleeve as she slid off her backpack. She cradled it in her arms, suddenly feeling protective and more than a bit wary of discussing its contents.

Of all the things she resented about her situation, the worst was having to think of everyone as a potential bad guy. She'd spent a good deal of her early adult life around top-clearance-oriented work and had always thought the stress of being responsible for the safety of top-secret information would be the tough part.

She now knew it didn't hold a candle to the mental and physical exhaustion of having to examine everything and everyone down to the tiniest little detail, searching for any clue that might indicate that they could harm her. Kill her.

She tightened her grip on the backpack. The shop was small and the shelves were low, so it was easy to determine that they were the only patrons there at the moment. Cali was certain Mr. Quéval had peeked to see who his customers were, just as she was certain that upon discovering they weren't islanders, he would likely not make an immediate appearance. The last thing he'd want to do was appear in any way eager to please. Heaven forbid.

John walked to the one and only checkout counter and lifted his hand to tap the bell there. Cali grabbed his wrist just in time. His skin was warm and her fingertips had landed directly on his pulse. It was strong and rapid. She let go immediately.

He shot her a questioning look.

"He knows we're here. You'll only slow him down if you ring that."

"Right," he said with mock solemnity. "How silly of me."

"You? Silly? Not in this lifetime." He frowned, and she wished she hadn't teased him. He might rile up more than her temper, but it wouldn't kill the guy to have a friend. It wouldn't hurt her right now, either.

She began strolling the first aisle, picking out a bottle of sunscreen and a box of Band-Aids. She was back by the aspirin shelf when John caught up to her.

"We don't have time to go shopping, Cali."

"If you want to use the darkroom you do."

"Ah." He leaned forward and selected a box of cotton swabs and a bottle of alcohol, adding it to her handbasket. "Mercenary mercantile."

She ducked her head and grinned. He made what was happening seem almost normal, putting a weird all-in-a-day's-work spin on it. Which, for him, was probably the case. "Something like that," she murmured, adding a few small tins of tart fruit candy to the lot. Passion fruit, she noticed as she glanced down. She stifled a sigh.

"Is there a certain required combination here, or can we just empty a shelf and get on with it?"

"No. No real rhyme or reason. I think this will do." She quickly stepped around him and headed to the front. Without turning, she said, "You know, you're cute when you get impatient."

His footsteps paused on the cracked linoleum floor. "What did you say?"

She began humming. Having a friend couldn't hurt right now, she thought again. Trying to be McShane's friend, however, might kill her. But as a distraction from her other worries, it was as good a ploy as any. He'd get used to the idea. Eventually.

He caught up to her. "Cali—"

"*Bonjour* . . . Monsieur Quéval?" she called out, deliberately cutting him off. One at a time she unloaded the items in her handbasket onto the narrow, worn linoleum counter.

John leaned in and eased the backpack from the crook of her arm. She tightened her elbow to her side instinctively. He lifted a brow in silent question, making her cheeks warm a bit. She let go.

"Sorry. Reflex. I guess you *are* one of the good guys."

He unzipped the bag, slid the binder inside, closed it, and slung it carefully over one shoulder. His gaze never left hers. "I have my moments."

His intent stare made her hands pause in mid-motion. Before she could comment, the proprietor made his grand entrance.

Wiping his hands on the white lab coat he wore, Mr. Quéval shambled slowly to the counter. His gait was that of a large man with a very low center of gravity. Since he was short and wiry, it was almost comical to watch him. She'd talked with him several times and each time had been almost disappointed that his accent was a lilting native Creole and not the nasal Brooklyn twang that would have suited him perfectly.

"Busy day?" she asked brightly.

"Not particularly."

Cali smiled through gritted teeth. "Lucky us, then, to have your services all to ourselves."

"A little thick, don't you think?"

John's whisper barely reached her ears as he bent to adjust the backpack. Still she noticed Mr. Quéval's attention drift, seemingly unconcerned, to her partner.

Quéval was second only to Eudora in the busybody department. Unfortunately, it was twice as hard to get information from him, which was to say impossible. John moved next to her. *Go ahead*, she wanted to say, *I dare you to charm this man*.

She shifted back slightly, urging him forward. This she wanted to see. As if he'd read her thoughts, John shot her a devastating smile, which he smoothly shifted to include Quéval.

Quéval smiled back.

My oh my, Cali thought, resisting the urge to fan herself. So she'd underestimated him. Again. In this case it was a bet well worth losing. Boy, to be on the receiving end of that lightning-bolt smile on a regular basis . . .

"*Bonjour,*" John said, extending his hand. "John McShane. I'm a photographer with an American television station." He spoke in French. The American version, but close enough to the island dialect to impress both her and Quéval, even if he didn't show it. Cali just barely caught her mouth from dropping open at his surprising linguistic ability.

The older man ignored his outstretched hand and just sniffed. Cali tucked her chin to keep from laughing and made a production out of emptying the rest of the basket. Smart-ass. She should be more upset that he could blow their only chance at uncovering Nathan's invisible notes. She doubted he failed often, and she had a front-row seat. She really shouldn't be enjoying herself.

She set the empty basket on the floor, stifling another smile.

She supposed she should rescue him, try to salvage what was left of their chances. John spoke before the thought became deed.

He gracefully tucked his hand in the pocket of his shorts and pulled out a folded piece of paper. "Actually," he said, still in French, staring at the note as if reminding himself of their contents. "I'm here on an advance scouting shoot."

The shop owner looked alarmed and bored at the same time. Only Quéval could pull that one off.

"You shoot things?"

"With a camera," John said.

Quéval looked only bored now. He turned to Cali's purchases, slowly lifting each one, looking carefully for the price—which she was certain he'd long memorized—and keying it into an old-fashioned cash register with precise punches.

The old McShane charm wouldn't work with this old fox. John could learn the island dialect. He couldn't not be an American.

"I'm with the Worldwide Television Network," he persisted.

Cali thought about kicking him in the shins to shut him up. His easy banter sounded so natural. He also sounded totally sincere. He must have done very well in super-spy school, she thought cynically, beginning to wonder if that smile was only pulled out for job-related purposes.

"You may know of us. We produce that soap opera, *Many Loves, Many Lives.*"

Looking away, Cali rolled her eyes, then stepped forward. Enough was enough. She would have gladly handed him more rope to hang himself with just for the sake of having future ammunition, but there was no time. She froze in mid-step when Quéval dropped the sunscreen. He attempted to cover his interest, but it was too late.

"So, what is your interest here?" Quéval asked.

Cali's gaze swung to the shopkeeper. He still

sounded as bored and uncaring as he looked. But Cali knew better. Not only had he willingly invited conversation, he'd done so in flawless English.

John grinned easily. "We film some of our episodes overseas. My job is to fly around, find suitable locations, take some advance shots, and send them back to the main office in New York City."

"You want to make *Many Loves, Many Lives* here in Aleria?" All pretense of boredom was gone.

Cali leaned back against the counter and folded her arms. "I bow before the master," she muttered. But no one was listening to her.

"Well, see, I sort of got myself into a bind. I became so excited when I stumbled onto your village here that I went a little crazy and I don't have enough chemicals to process all my shots." He moved over and slung an arm around Cali's shoulders. "Madame Ellis was kind enough to tell me all about your studio."

She tried to mask her surprise at the unexpected physical contact. She aimed a wide smile at Monsieur Quéval. "I knew you were the one man who could help him." John's fingers tightened slightly. He moved closer, bumping his hip along her waist.

"You want me to develop your film?" Quéval asked.

"Actually, I was hoping I could rent your darkroom for an hour or two," John replied smoothly.

That set Quéval back. Wariness and suspicion entered his eyes once again.

John reached in his back pocket and took out his wallet.

Shaking his head, Quéval raised a warning finger. "American dollars—"

"I have francs."

Cali was getting used to being held against McShane's big warm body, telling herself she shouldn't feel each contact point so intensely, but a part of her was still focused on the transaction. First, island dialect. Now francs.

"Magna cum laude in super-secret spy school," she said under her breath. "Either that or you were a helluva Boy Scout."

"What was that?" John turned slightly, angling her against his body far too naturally.

"Boy Scouts?" Quéval questioned.

Cali smiled brightly. His smooth moves might irritate her, but there was too much riding on this to blow it. "I said, 'Boy, scouting can be hell.' "

He looked skeptical, but John didn't give him a chance to think on it.

"My budget isn't unlimited," he said, steering the conversation back to the one subject guaranteed to hold Quéval's interest. He uncurled a wad of colorful bills. "But I think I can pay your price."

Cali almost snorted at the cupidity dripping from the shopkeeper's tongue. Yes, her life was in danger, yes, her adrenal glands had surpassed themselves in production days ago. But she was actually enjoying the rush. With McShane at her side, she felt . . . invincible.

She directed her attention from Quéval to John. His winning smile said he was quite used to getting what he wanted and that he was quite willing to pay for it.

Yet she felt his muscles grow tighter as he awaited Quéval's decision. Her hand crept to his waist. She pressed her fingers into his side. It wasn't until he squeezed her shoulder in return that she realized she'd tried to reassure him. It pleased her more than a little to know that she could.

Quéval named a price. Cali gulped. John relaxed against her, though she was certain only she knew it.

He stuck out his hand. *"Merci beaucoup."*

Mr. Quéval's hand remained palm up. She felt John stifle a sigh and again felt the urge to laugh. He removed his arm from her shoulder and peeled off a large number of bills.

She frowned at the sudden feeling of abandonment. She'd adapted to his touch, his close proximity, far too easily. His arm snaked smoothly around her waist once again as he spoke. She moved closer, fitting against him. All part of the act, she told herself.

Liar.

John went to place the money in the shopkeeper's outstretched hand, but withheld it at the last second. "Is the darkroom available now by any chance?"

It was obvious Quéval didn't like being cornered so smoothly, but his eyes never left the stack of bills hovering over his fingertips. Greed won. He gave a sharp nod. *"Oui."* He all but snatched the money as soon as it grazed his skin, swiftly counting it.

John's easy smile had never so much as flickered during the entire transaction. There was no hint of triumph, just genuine appreciation.

"Thanks." John turned and stepped toward to the end of the counter. "I'll leave everything as I find it."

In one smooth move, Mr. Quéval pocketed the money, shifted his attention to Cali, and said, "That will be one hundred twenty-five francs, please."

Momentarily nonplussed, Cali just stared at him. Right. Her purchases. John didn't shift so much as a hair, but Cali sensed he was enjoying the moment immensely. Valiantly striving to match his easy grace, she pasted on her most sincere smile and slipped out from under John's arm to dig in her backpack.

She handed over the plain green-and-white bills, smiling sweetly as he grumbled, "American." She moved back to John's side, looked over her shoulder, and said, "You can just box them up for me and set them by the door. Thanks."

She had to duck her head to hide her smug grin at Quéval's affronted sniff . . . even as he lifted a box from behind the counter.

"Always pushing it." John's voice barely touched her ears.

She turned her head slightly, placing her mouth close to his jaw. "I'm a quick study."

"I got us a darkroom, didn't I?"

John pushed open the door, but Cali stopped him with a hand on his arm. "Where in the world did you come up with the television angle?"

John pulled Cali back a step and pointed to the

back room. A small color television was blaring; the people on the screen were familiar American actors, their speech obviously dubbed into French. It was a soap opera.

"*As the World Turns.*"

She looked at him. "So?"

"It comes on right after *Many Loves, Many Lives.* He didn't come to the desk until it was over."

"Sometimes you're so good, you scare me."

He gifted her with a bright flash of a smile, then ushered her into the lab. He closed the door, locked it, tested the lock, then turned to her. "Show time."

She was prepared for smugness, had a retort all ready, but gone was the smiling, affable man. The man before her was all business. From his "no fooling around" stance, to his cool "let's get down to it" gray eyes.

Cali frowned, the unease and tension crawled back into her.

He paused. "Something wrong?"

She pulled the backpack off and unzipped it. "You make a great Indiana Jones, but I'm no good as Joan Wilder."

"You're mixing your adventure movies."

She pulled out the notebook and placed it on the counter next to them. "Sue me."

John stepped closer, pushed the notebook aside, and cupped her shoulders. Cali stiffened.

"Don't fall apart on me now. You're doing better than most people would in your position."

His praise, faint as it was, meant far too much. "Gee, thanks. I feel so much better now."

He looked affronted. Actually, he looked confused and a little bit hurt, but that couldn't be.

"I'm sorry," she said, sincere. "I just don't do real well on weeklong rollercoaster rides. I want to turn in my E ticket now if you don't mind." She'd been aiming for flippant. Instead she'd simply sounded defeated. *Wonderful Cali, inspire even more respect. The man is risking his life for you, after all. Get with it.* She straightened her spine.

His fingers dug into her shoulders, then began a slow massage. "You ready to take a peek inside that notebook?" His tone was even, but his touch was soothing. And somewhere in those eyes was something very much like tenderness.

She stepped away from his touch. Maybe taking on McShane as a friend wasn't such a good idea after all.

She pasted a determined look on her face. "Yes. Once we know what it is we're dealing with, then maybe we'll know who the good guys are. Call them in, hand over this stuff, arrange a little short-term protection while they round up the bad guys, and"— she snapped her fingers—"voilà, all better."

"Cali—"

She lifted a hand. "It's my fantasy, I worked hard devising one I could believe in for more than thirty seconds. Let me hold on to it for at least another hour or two, okay?"

John reached out and ran a finger down the side of her jaw.

There *was* tenderness in John McShane.

She told herself that what she needed was his strength. He'd been her anchor during the most turbulent period of her life. She realized now that had he shown her any tenderness then, she'd have fallen completely apart. What she'd needed was his solid-as-a-rock support, his unfailing invulnerability. A man impervious to any weakness.

The man touching her now was not remotely weak. However, she wasn't so sure about the vulnerability.

It scared her to think he might need an occasional anchor too. It scared her to think he might need that from her. It terrified her to realize she wanted to give it to him. If he let her.

She lifted her hand and covered his. His skin was dry and warm, his steady pulse far too reassuring. "I do appreciate all you're doing for me, John." She dropped her hand and stepped away. Her smile was tremulous but real. "Ready whenever you are."

John looked as if he were about to say something, but instead turned off the bright overhead then flipped on the red safelight.

She scanned the room, refamiliarizing herself with the process and equipment. It had been too long. "I'm not sure I remember enough." She handed him the notebook.

He locked eyes with her, the red light enhancing the sudden ferocity in his strangely transparent-looking gaze.

"This may not work," he said. "If it doesn't—"

"Then the pages could really be blanks. Let's not think about—"

"You have to think about it, Cali. If there is no help here, grilling Eudora isn't really a great alternative. The people after you are too well funded, too connected, though I'll be damned if I can figure out how. We don't have time. For all we know, they are on their way here right now. If we can't decipher Nathan's notes here on Martinique, then one or both of us will have to look elsewhere."

The idea of him leaving her panicked her. "I go where you go." She'd sounded more forceful than she'd liked, but if her sudden vehemence surprised him, he didn't show it.

"Fine." He turned his complete attention to the notebook. Subject closed. She couldn't decide if she was relieved that he wouldn't abandon her to take up the fight alone at the first sign of a problem, or annoyed that he'd so easily dismissed her concerns.

Shoving the whole mental merry-go-round aside, she stepped over to the trays, looking at the rows of chemicals. Bleach, stabilizers, potassium iodide wash, conditioner. The French labels translated fairly easily. Quéval was no amateur. To her surprise, she found the processes coming back to her as she went over all the equipment. "Like riding a bike." She snagged some graduated beakers and went about setting everything up as best as she could, then stepped up behind

John and watched over his shoulder. He carefully flipped open the rings and slid out the first blank page.

She checked the temperature of the liquid, realizing as she did so that she had no idea if what was appropriate for processing film worked on invisible ink. "We can skip the first few steps since this isn't film. Even so, the way we're doing this is a bit unorthodox."

"I'm not sure it matters."

"We're about to find out." Satisfied as she could be, she took one sheet and slipped it into the first tray.

"Nothing," he said.

"Be patient." But she felt her own pulse rocketing faster. She willed her hands to be steady as she agitated the tray to keep the developer evenly distributed. She gently rapped the tray on the table to dislodge bubbles that were attaching to the surface.

"There's something there!" She hadn't really let herself believe it until that moment. She leaned over, squinting. Some of it was handwritten margin notes, but the bulk of it was typed. It all glowed an odd yellow, making it almost impossible to decipher in the red light.

She glanced around. Quéval kept an orderly darkroom. She located what she sought almost immediately. John had nudged into her spot.

"Here," she said, handing him a small magnifier. "See if this helps."

"Can you make any of it out?"

He was silent just long enough for her to wonder if he'd forgotten she was there.

"Yes. I can."

His tone was flat and emotionless. Normal, in other words. And yet she stilled, a sense of dread creeping over her.

"Tell me, John. What is it?"

"Do another sheet, Cali." He handed her the page that followed the one she'd already done.

She complied. He studied that one silently. "One more."

"What is it?"

He handed her another sheet. "Do this one."

She huffed out an impatient sigh, but did as he asked, knowing he wouldn't tell her anything until he was ready.

After studying the third page for several long minutes, John laid down the magnifier and turned to her. "You'll have to go over this. And we'll need much more information. A lot more. Monsieur Quéval's time and supplies won't be nearly enough."

"Just tell me what you suspect."

"These pages are outline notes. Your husband created a virus program. The diskettes apparently contain the actual program work. All encrypted. I'm not sure if his code notes are here or not."

"Virus protection programs are incredibly sophisticated these days. A ten-year-old virus could hardly be a threat."

"This one is."

"How so?"

"I'm not the computer wiz, that's your job. So you'll have to verify this for me." He pulled her closer and handed her the magnifier.

"For God's sake, can't you just tell me?"

He turned her to the table. "See it for yourself, Cali." He pointed halfway down the page. "Read that."

She bent over the table and peered through the lens. "You are the most insufferable . . ." The words died away on a sudden inhalation. "Oh my God. No." She stood up, the magnifier hanging limply in her hand. "Nathan, what did you do?" she whispered.

"He created a virus that can dismantle entire computer networks," John said, confirming what she already knew. "And from what I can tell, it works with the detection codes so when a protection program kicks in, the virus is automatically activated."

Cali turned wide eyes to him as the bigger picture clicked into place. "And if it's set up properly today, the sender could retrieve all the file names and access codes as the detection program scanned them." She swore under her breath. "Imagine what someone with this could do to, say, a bank?"

In a deceptively soft voice, John added, "Imagine what someone with this could do to, say, an entire government."

SIX

Even in the red glow John saw Cali's skin pale.

"The bank alone was worth killing for." Her eyes widened. She turned to him. "I'm a dead woman."

"No."

He'd almost shouted. He knew how intimidating he could be. Cali didn't even blink. Her mind was spinning out on just what she'd gotten herself into.

"I don't have the actual program," she said.

He didn't remind her of the diskettes that were in the package. "We do have Nathan's notes. And if the first page is any indication, the entire history of the program up to his death is all contained in here."

She focused on him. He wished she hadn't. There was resignation in her eyes. He wanted to shake her.

"You're a fighter, Cali. You made it this far—"

"Yeah, with this stupid, wide-eyed notion of avenging Nathan. Instead I'm going to end up just like him. Dead."

"Knowledge is power, Cali. We can use this to our advantage. The same information that could kill you will be your ticket out."

She planted her hands on her hips. "They tried to kill me without knowing how much I knew or what I had. I could destroy this notebook and they wouldn't stop. I could turn it over to them and I would still be signing my death warrant. I know too much."

"What happened to your plan?"

"Give it to the good guys, you mean? I don't even know who they are anymore." Her hands fell limply to her sides. "I'm sorry. I guess I'm just not up to saving the world as we know it."

It was a toss-up which he clenched tighter, his jaw or his hands. He wanted to protect her and at the same time her acquiescence irritated him. He'd bullied her out of giving in once before. He wasn't sure he was up to the task again. He already cared too much. She'd look at him, all wounded and defiant at the same time, sticking her chin up but fully expecting to be punched. She'd suck him under again.

"There are no good guys," she said quietly. "This program is designed to destroy." She lifted those damnable eyes to him, and he felt the undertow tugging at his feet. "I can't give this to anyone, John. I'd never be able to live with myself." She laughed, but the sound was hollow. "Not that this will be a concern for much longer."

He took her shoulders, pulling her upright until her chin bobbed just below his.

"Listen to me, dammit." His fingers tightened

when her expression remained dead. "First off, there are good guys out there. I left a handful of them to traipse over here to rescue your backside."

A bit of fire crept back in. "Well please, by all means go back to them." She tried to shrug away, but he held her fast.

"Yeah, well, we all have better things to do than risk our butts for you, especially now." That stoked the fire. Good. "But I can round up someone. We need to find out who wants this information. I doubt there is only one faction involved, or you would have been taken out already."

"If you think you are giving me any hope here, you are way off the mark, McShane. I may have taken your bullying ten years ago, but not this time."

She redoubled her efforts to pull away. He held on, shaking her gently. "Then don't waste my time and yours by making me play bully again."

"You're not playing, you are a bully." She shot a meaningful look at his tight grip on her shoulders.

He softened his hold, but not his expression. "I agreed to take this assignment on. I don't fail, Cali."

She snorted, "Well, golly gee, we can't have that. I'm sure if we just send that over in a note to the other side, they'll withdraw. Let me go."

"Not until you get off this martyr shtick."

"I'm simply being a realist."

"We're wasting time, Cali."

"We already know what we've got."

"We only know enough to get us killed. But you can only get so dead. We need as much info as we can get. I want to scan through and see if the program itself is written down anywhere. If what's been done is on the diskettes you have, you'll have to get into them and see if you can find out as much as possible without triggering the damn thing."

"Where do you propose we do this?"

"We should try to decipher as much of the written work as we can. Our next step is getting out of here and getting somewhere safe."

"We've been over this."

"Both of us, Cali. Like I said, this definitely constitutes calling in my team." He tapped on the open page of the binder. "We have proof now. Or at least we will."

"John, I don't know if we should contact any-one—"

"It's okay. We don't know all the players or their agendas, but I do know my team. They only have one agenda."

"But they still answer to someone. And that some-one might have an agenda."

"As it happens, that isn't the case."

Cali paused, then said, "What aren't you telling me?"

She was getting far too good at reading him. Or he was getting far too sloppy in allowing her to. "Nothing that makes a difference right now. But if you trust me, you can trust them."

"So do we decipher it? Leave the island? To go back to the States? And what about the photo? Nathan had it in there for a reason. We haven't found anything more here."

"I don't think we need to. Because of the separate security boxes, I doubt Nathan intended for you ever to get hold of the entire thing. Maybe the photo was a lead, somehow. But we have it now. We discovered what the program is for, that's all we need."

"There is one thing we don't have."

"Which is?"

"A playing roster of the good guys and bad guys. Maybe that is what we were supposed to find here."

"True, but we don't have time to waste trying to acquire one. My instincts are screaming at me to get us both off this island."

"What's the success rate of your instincts?"

It was on the tip of his tongue to say one hundred percent. But he was staring at the one person who'd lowered his average. Where Cali was concerned, John questioned everything, especially his instincts. "Enough that I'm here to help you now."

She shook her head. "I don't know, McShane. Your instincts say to go into hiding. Mine say there is something here, something that will help us."

John stepped closer. "Whatever that something is won't help us if we're dead. And we're not hiding. If it helps you put it in perspective, we aren't just getting out of sight. While my guys work to put together that playing roster, you are going to spend some time in front of a computer screen trying to figure out exactly how this virus works. And, if you can, how to circumvent it. That will be our trump card."

"You do think they're on the way, then. You think Eudora tipped them off to my whereabouts when I took the package?"

"Eudora has always known your whereabouts. I think she is just a messenger, possibly an innocent one."

"Eudora is no fool. No way would she do anyone a favor without knowing exactly what was going on." She waved a hand. "Besides, even if Eudora was just an innocent messenger, why give that package to me? Certainly if they'd intercepted this from Grand Cayman, they knew what they had. They could have found someone in their employ to decode it."

"They couldn't before, when you gave them the notes and disk from the first deposit box, assuming that's what they really were. They must have decided to send it on and let you do all the hard work for them." John straightened and gathered up the binder. "We need to get out of here, Cali. Now."

Cali tried not to react to the sudden urgency in his tone. She felt as if she'd ridden the world's steepest roller coaster at warp speed. Her analytical mind was begging for time to sort through all the information she'd dumped into it. She also didn't realize until that moment that she'd veered from terror over the certainty that she was going to die, to hope that a way out of this mess was possible after all. And even if they couldn't find a way out, there was no loss in believing there was one until the last moment.

What else did she have to hold on to?

She looked at John. She had John—he was the source of her hope.

"Okay. What do we do? Where do we go?"

He was sliding the binder in her backpack, but he paused to look at her. "Did you just agree to do something without an argument?"

"I'm sure I'll make up for it later." There was a hint of something underneath his gibe. It sounded far too much like concern. Hope she needed, strength she needed. Concern and tenderness from John she didn't need right now. It made her want to surrender what control she had to him, give herself entirely over to his very reliable, more than capable hands. It made her feel weak.

And weakness was the one thing she definitely could not risk. Not now. Not ever.

She turned away and went about cleaning up. She carefully disposed of the used chemicals and returned everything to its place.

Even her plans for a distracting attempt at friendship were beginning to look like a fool's endeavor. She was coming to understand that any relationship with John McShane would not be done in half measures.

Once the sheet was passably dry, she protected it in a cover, then went to the door, flipped off the safelight, and turned the regular light back on. The sudden brightness made her squeeze her eyes shut. "What are we going to tell Quéval?"

From a point way inside her personal space, he said, "Nothing."

She slowly opened her eyes. He was standing right in front of her. He reached for her. She braced herself for his touch, not having enough time to raise her defenses after her little internal assessment of her relationship with John.

It never came. Instead his hand went past her to the light switch. She automatically groped behind her for the doorknob as the small room was plunged into complete darkness.

"Now, *this* is a darkroom." Her nervous laugh fell into the silence.

"I thought you had the door."

"I do." And an overactive imagination too. She found the knob and started to turn. His hand fell unerringly on her shoulder. She stilled.

"Cali—" His voice was rougher. Or maybe it just vibrated differently in the dark. He paused, then made a small sound, as if he was clearing his throat. Her own throat tightened.

"What?" She barely squeezed the word out.

"I, uh . . ."

John McShane, stuttering? She didn't know whether to be alarmed or flattered. In reality, she was both. "What's wrong, McShane?" Using his last name didn't establish the critical distance she needed to feel from him right at that moment. She wasn't sure anything would have.

"You really are handling this—all of this—well."

She exhaled, certain that wasn't what he'd been about to say, but nonetheless relieved that he had. "Thanks," she tossed off. She twisted the knob again.

"Nathan would be proud of you, Cali."

Her hand slid off the knob. She made some noise in her throat that was supposed to sound like a reply, but it was all tangled up in the emotions rising inside her at the sincerity in his quietly spoken words.

"Thank you, John," she finally managed.

She felt his hand on her shoulder like a brand. His fingers tightened for a moment, then the pressure was gone. The warmth from his palm dissipated too quickly. She wanted to grab at his hand, put it back on her body. Better yet, how easy it would be to turn a fraction and press her entire length against his long, hard, warm frame. Security, strength, compassion. She knew he possessed all three. But that wasn't what was making her skin tingle in anticipation, wasn't what was making her pulse race or her palms moist.

Perhaps it was simply the turmoil that caused her to think about him as more than a skilled aide. But she quickly realized her attraction to one John McShane, super-secret spy, went beyond his job description or her need for his services in that capacity.

"We'd better get back to the bungalow."

Her eyes had adjusted to the dark. He was big and close, his body angled to hers in a way that made her feel protected.

She turned. "Yeah, I guess we should."

"Cali—"

He broke off. She didn't rush to fill the silence. Instead she let it expand, deepen, until it, along with the darkness, enveloped them both like a cocoon.

He gently cupped her shoulders. She couldn't repress the shiver his touch sent racing over her. The coolness was a delicious counterpoint to the sudden coil of heat expanding inside her.

"John." Her voice was throaty and rough. She didn't back away this time. It made her feel as if she was vibrating from the inside out.

His hand drifted from her shoulder to her neck. She turned her cheek into his palm as his hand slid higher.

He stepped in closer. She let him.

Somewhere inside her head a little voice was screaming caution, telling her she didn't need to get further involved with him.

But every other cell in her body was screaming that this was exactly what she needed. It was sure as hell what she wanted.

He rubbed his thumb across her lower lip. Her long sigh was low and broken, ending on a soft moan. "John."

"Cali." Her name was a warm, fresh breath across her lips. She parted them.

She'd expected his lips to be firm, the kiss to be hard and formidable, like the man. So she was completely undone by the soft, wet feel of his lips, the gentle way his mouth cushioned hers, giving more than taking.

"Oh," she sighed, easing more fully into his kiss, wanting more of the unexpected, yet sweet succor she'd found there.

He let her deepen the kiss, his lips parting to take her mouth more fully. He allowed her a slow, thorough exploration of his mouth, letting the kiss slowly build steam. Then he took the same liberty. She marveled at his almost painstaking patience. He made love to her mouth as if it were her entire body. And, in fact, her entire body was reacting. His control steadily eroded hers, until the pressure of the contained steam between them was of volcanic proportions.

She pressed her hands to his chest, feeling the evidence of what his control was costing him. His heart was pounding every bit as hard as hers. He lifted his mouth slightly on a long sigh. She felt it all the way to her suddenly wobbly knees. She slid her hands to his shoulders, holding on for support. His grip tightened too.

"You have no idea how long I've wanted to do that."

His whispered words filtered slowly into the haze that was her brain. There was something there, she thought almost dazedly, something that sounded almost confessional.

Further thought was abruptly interrupted by a short rap at the door. John jerked back as if he'd been branded. Cali had no time to think.

"You almost done in there?" It was Quéval.

"Yes. Be out in a second."

There was no missing the relief in his voice. That stung. Neither reaction made sense at the moment.

"Cali, I—"

The confusion and the sudden yank back to reality served to jump-start her control. She straightened her back and put a small but crucial bit of space between them.

"Don't." She looked into the shadow that was his face. There was nothing there to guide her. "Just let it go, okay?" She didn't wait for an answer, knowing McShane did whatever he damn well pleased. She wasn't remotely up to the task of finding out what pleased him at the moment. She turned and opened the door to find Quéval all but pressed up against it. It made her wonder how long he'd been there.

Funneling irritation over the rush of emotions inside her toward Quéval was an easy out. She wasn't too proud to take it.

"I'm sorry, did you knock again?" she said with saccharine sweetness. "Thank you so much for your lab."

"The pictures, they are done? Can I see them?"

Cali opened her mouth to tell him that she was terribly sorry but the photos were too drab and dreary, but John, apparently reading her mood too well, smoothly stepped between them.

He nudged her firmly past Quéval, saying, "I think what I have here is great. I didn't want to waste your chemicals doing them all up. We're heading out of here right now."

Cali looked over her shoulder just as Quéval's eyes lit up. He'd been following John down the hallway, but stopped. "You're leaving the island?"

Cali noted that John picked up on the undercurrents immediately. His congenial smile never wavered as he turned back to the shopkeeper. "Why, yes. I think my search is over. I'm going to head straight back to the studios and get to work on a presentation. I'll develop them there. I appreciate your help."

"Your studio is in New York City?"

Cali felt rather than saw John tense. She hadn't missed his intentionally vague reference.

"We have both East and West Coast offices." He turned back down the hall, pushing Cali along in front of him. "Thanks again."

His pace wasn't rushed, but his grip on her arm told Cali that nothing was going to stop him until he was outside.

"You will let me know?" Quéval followed them down the hall, apparently so intent on getting information out of them that he was unconcerned over appearing anxious.

"Sure thing." John waved a hand over his head, then all but shoved Cali out the front door. "We've got less than an hour to get off this island," he said, his voice low and carrying only as far as her ear. He picked up his speed, causing her to stumble along beside him for a few steps.

She finally pulled away from him and stopped. "Can we slow down for a second?"

"No." He kept walking.

"We forgot my box of merchandise. John—" She broke off on a frustrated sigh and stormed after him. Her legs were average length, but she was almost trotting to maintain his pace. "Do you really think they are so close?"

"Breathing down our proverbial necks. Weren't you listening back there?"

"Of course. I know you purposely avoided telling him where we were heading. But that's just good common sense."

"Everything we said will be common knowledge very shortly."

"Oh, come on, he's a busybody, but the whole town isn't in on this conspiracy."

"Someone nearby is. Bet on it."

"Your super-secret"—she stopped when he glared at her—"spy instincts," she finished evenly. "I can get my stuff out of the bungalow in less than thirty minutes."

"No time for that. We're heading directly for the harbor."

"There has to be time." She stopped. "Harbor?" He kept on walking. She had to dash to catch up to him. She grabbed his elbow. "Slow down, or I'll pass out before we get anywhere." He did. Marginally. "John, I have to go back to the bungalow. Five minutes. Just let me get a few things. It's important."

"You can get whatever you need when we get off the island."

"I'm not talking about cosmetics and a treasured blouse, McShane." She yanked on his arm. "For God's sake, slow down!" It was like trying to stop a train with a handcart. She let go and abruptly stopped, crossing her arms. The path to the bungalow forked ahead. He strode another dozen yards before finally slowing then stopping. He looked up, sighed, then turned to face her.

"Whatever it is can't be worth your life."

Calmly, she said, "What I want is all I have left of my life."

John stared at her for an eternal moment, then turned toward the path leading to the bungalow. "Five minutes." He didn't look back to see if she followed.

Cali refused to run, but she did catch up with him as they hit the front walk. She stepped on the deck in front of him and turned at the door. "Thank you. It's just some photos and the stuff in my purse. But it's all of me I have left."

"Just hurry."

She frowned. Where was the tender, compassionate man who'd kissed her so thoroughly? "I'll be out in two." She slipped through the screen and headed straight to the small bedroom. She heard the door tap the frame and John's soft tread on the floor. She felt rather than heard him in the doorway behind her. She tossed the backpack on the bed and opened the single small drawer on the wicker nightstand. "Eudora will have a field day wondering where I went when she comes to get the flowers. At least I paid her up front. I'd feel awful if—" She was rambling. Nerves. She took several steady breaths. John remained silent. It didn't help much. He made an impressive sentry.

She scooped the contents of the drawer into the backpack then snagged a handful of shorts, tees, and underwear from the wardrobe. "I could throw this in a suitcase and—"

"Keep it light, only what you can carry."

"Fine." She hit the small bathroom and dumped her cosmetics bag in. She thought she heard John sigh but wasn't sure. She smiled. "Hey, it was here, I was here. You never know when you might need kohl eyeliner while dodging bullets. Could come in handy."

John scowled. She'd been hoping for a reaction. That hadn't been it. "Okay, okay. Done. Let's go."

She got to the doorway but he didn't budge. "Well?"

The tension emanating from him was almost a visual aura. "Cali, there are some things you should know. In case anything happens to me. Who to contact."

"Give it to me on the boat. I assume that is the desired method of travel?" She spoke quickly, not wanting to entertain even for a moment the thought that anything could happen to him. "Come on." She went to push past him. He stopped her. She didn't look at him. "McShane, you've been yelling at me about how much of a hurry we're in. Let's go."

"I don't yell."

His answer had her turning to him without conscious thought. "Wha—"

The slapping of the screen door brought an abrupt end to her question.

SEVEN

John grabbed Cali and pressed her to the wall behind the bedroom door, flattening his body against hers. "Don't move, don't even whisper." His words were hot and urgent, his lips pressed directly on her earlobe. She nodded.

John locked his gaze on hers as he backed slowly away. He watched her eyes widen when he slipped his hand to the small of his back and retrieved a fully loaded, fully automatic handgun. He watched her skin pale and her throat work. *Stay with me*, *Cali*, he urged silently, holding her gaze by sheer will. As if he'd spoken, she slowly nodded. Adrenaline hammering through him, he winked his approval, tried for a reassuring smile, then turned his full attention to the front entry.

Angling his body, he peered through the slit between the door and the frame. He swore silently as a tall figure moved into view. It was no one he knew, but the man had definitely been to Uncle Sam's super-spy school. Cali's time had just run out.

The only exit open to them was the window over the bed. Unfortunately the old rattan headboard half covered the lower screened-in portion. The man crept into the kitchen.

John moved back to Cali, pressing his mouth against her ear. "We go out the window. I'll get the screen out, you go out first. Don't wait for me. Run uphill and bury yourself in the biggest bush you can find." It was a calculated risk that they'd sent only one agent. But until he had a chance to find out, good cover in that jungle she called a garden was their best hope. "Run fast, Cali, and don't look back. I'll find you."

She nodded. Their time to escape undetected had passed. He knew they'd be lucky to clear the window.

It had been totally unprofessional of him to let her come back there. Now they might pay for that unpardonable mistake with their lives. He'd broken rule number one—don't form any attachments.

Cali grabbed his arm. He spun back and shook his head hard. No time, he mouthed silently. She shook her head just as fiercely then pointed to the bathroom. There was no window in there. Which meant she wanted something. Frowning, he shook his head again, intentionally looking as formidable as he could, which was a fair amount if his colleagues and previous rescue targets were to be believed.

The sound of the back screen door creaking stilled them both for a split second. He pulled away and moved as silently as possible to the headboard. At the right angle, he could be easily viewed from the main room. But from the kitchen, the intruder would have to be square in the doorway to see him. He heard a bare whisper of sound behind him and spun, weight centered, ready.

It was Cali. She was heading for the bathroom, easing the backpack straps onto her shoulders. In two strides he was in front of her. What in the hell was she doing? Anger coursed through him, fear was a close second. The two emotions combined put him closer to going over the edge than he'd ever been before. The threat of losing all control helped him focus. *Get her out alive. Then throttle her.*

Just as his hand closed around her wrist she pointed up. Set into the bathroom ceiling was a screened vent with a crank handle to lift the louvered cover. He made the decision in an instant. He shoved her inside, silently closed the bathroom door, then grabbed her face and kissed her hard on the mouth. "You just saved your life."

She grabbed his face and kissed him back. She grinned. "Yours too. Let's move."

Too stunned to do anything else, he released her, immediately stepped up on the small vanity, and opened the glass panel. The screen came out easily. He pushed it out onto the roof, then cupped his hands as Cali climbed onto the lid of the commode. She slid the pack off, and John slung one strap over his shoulder. Then she grabbed his shoulders to steady herself and put her foot in his hand.

As he went to lift her she captured his gaze. She wasn't smiling now. Her eyes burned holes into him, sending messages he didn't have time to interpret. He lifted her, and she disappeared gracefully through the open frame.

He could feel the proximity of the agent like hot breath on his neck. Terror crept right along with it, scuttling down his spine. A sudden vision of Cali running and a single bullet taking her to the ground almost paralyzed him. Instincts far more ingrained than these new emotions roiling through him kicked in, and he hoisted the pack to her waiting hand, then jumped up and grabbed the edge of the frame.

As he pulled his feet through the hole he heard their intruder enter the bedroom behind him. That the agent was unconcerned about making noise was a good sign. His instincts were telling him the house was empty.

John intended to make the agent's rusty instincts prove correct.

Cali was already standing. He was beside her an instant later, his hand on her shoulder keeping her from moving. The weight of their first step would likely give them away, so he quickly scanned the roof for the most direct route down.

She pulled on his arm, then pointed to the back of the house, over the kitchen. "A shed," she whispered. He didn't wait; he grabbed her hand and made a bee-line for the back of the roof. They hopped down on the shed roof, but before Cali could turn to jump down the sloped front, John jumped off the side, putting the shed between them and the back door, then motioned for her to jump down to him.

He caught her easily against him. In that split instant he gave in to the overwhelming need to kiss her one more time, not wanting to acknowledge that he took the risk because he might never hold her again. It was far too brief and nothing like the tender taste he'd wanted.

"Run, Cali. Don't look back." Giving her no time to argue, he shoved her in front of him, pointed uphill, and said, "Now!"

To her credit, she took off like a bullet, getting herself behind the first tree then darting uphill. John had covered the back door in case the agent came out before she got clear. Satisfied now that she would do as he'd instructed, John flattened his back against the wall and edged to the opposite corner.

Where are you? "Come out, come out wherever you are," he sang under his breath. He wanted to neutralize the threat. In a perfect world, that meant incapacitating the intruder and drilling all the information out of him. But if silencing him permanently was the only way, he wasn't opposed to that either. John was pragmatic. It was a "him or me" world. He didn't waste time worrying about why the "him" did what he did. He just made sure when the dust cleared it was the "me" left standing.

He crept along the side wall of the bungalow, ducking under low, razor-edged palm fronds, then crouching at the front corner. The fact that the agent hadn't immediately pursued them was not a good sign. They hadn't left anything behind. And they'd crossed the roof with speed, not stealth, in mind. There was no way the agent could be unaware of their presence.

Where in the hell are you? John was getting a very bad feeling about this. Had they positioned someone uphill? Had the agent been sharper than John had given him credit for? Had he purposely let them know he was there in order to flush them out the back, knowing the jungle behind the bungalow was their best bet for cover and therefore escape?

Escape that had been an illusion?

Instincts clamoring, feeling dangerously out of touch, he closed in silently on the porch. He moved up the steps and positioned himself, back flat to the wall, next to the screen door. He went in hard and fast, gun held two-fisted, directed first at the bedroom then at the kitchen doorway.

Nothing.

"Hell." He scanned each room thoroughly. The back door was closed. He doubted the agent had left that way. He'd gone out the front while John was overseeing Cali's safe escape. Safe. He swore loudly and fluently.

He all but ripped the back door from the hinges, then hit the tangled, weed-choked hill at a dead run.

He'd gone less than ten yards when a large shadow came out of nowhere, tackling him hard. The blow as he hit the hill stunned him. The one shortly after that to the back of his head put him to sleep.

❖━━━━━━━━❖

The air was warm and steamy, yet she shivered. *Where was he?* She refused to look at her watch again. It had been two hours since McShane had given her a hard shove and told her to run.

Cali waited behind a thick stand of palms and bird of paradise. How could there be such ugliness in a place of such exotic beauty? she thought. As a distraction, such speculation was useless. Once again she peered through the fronds. Her line of vision to the bungalow was severely limited, as she'd been afraid that the better she could see the bungalow, the better her pursuer could see her.

She was about fifty yards from the back door. She'd have gone farther but that would have plunged her into the thick vegetation she knew bordered on one of the small rain forests of Martinique's interior. She trusted John to find her, but only to a point. Once in there, she'd be lost.

She shifted the pack, which she'd switched to a front hold, its bulk resting on her chest. The continued adrenaline rush into her system was beginning to take its toll. Her stomach was pitching against her throat and there was a fine tremor in her hands she couldn't seem to control.

I'll find you. She heard his urgent command as clearly as if he still had his lips pressed against her ear. For the last half hour those words had echoed incessantly in her mind, trying to drown out her little voice, which was telling her something had gone wrong. Terribly wrong. *He's not coming.*

She wanted to whisper the words out loud. Maybe acknowledging the truth would return some of her control, help her stop shaking, give her courage to deal with the obvious. She was alone. Again. Just her and the bad guys.

The warm ground was damp and the dampness had long ago seeped into her shorts. The edges of the palm fronds tickled her forearms. She hugged the backpack tighter and shifted slowly and quietly onto her knees. She scanned the hill leading down to the back door for the hundredth time. Nothing.

What now, Cali? Did she stay put? There had been no activity at the bungalow since she'd squinted downhill through the fronds for the first time. During her mad dash, she thought she'd heard the swish of bodies crunching through the brush and tangle behind her, but hadn't dared look over her shoulder. Once she'd gotten settled and could hear something other than her own labored breathing, it had been quiet. *Too quiet*, her little voice put in again. It was getting harder and harder to ignore the facts.

Either John had abandoned her or he'd been caught. She couldn't believe the former. He was loyal to a fault. Her fingers were on her lips, tracing the memory of his kisses, before she realized her action. She felt the commitment in his last kiss. Had seen it in his eyes. No. He wouldn't leave her. Not willingly.

That left capture. Or worse. He wouldn't lead them to her, to the disks and the notebook. That she knew. Which meant right at that moment he was probably being subjected to—

"Stop it!" she ordered in a harsh whisper, even as she shuddered at the unavoidable mental picture. The bile pitched more violently against her throat. Food. The banana plantation that she passed on the way to the village stretched far back into the hills. She knew she should eat, not let her strength diminish. But even the thought of a piece of fresh fruit made her stomach roll.

Focus, Cali, focus. Her head told her to get off the island and track down someone on John's team, turn the disks, the notebook, and the search for John over to them. Even if she could get off the island unde-tected, she had no idea whom he was working for now. Or whom to ask.

Your father. No. She refused to get him involved, because it would be akin to handing control squarely back to him. But mostly she wanted to keep him safe. He was her only family, the only person left alive with whom she felt a connection. In fact, she'd wondered before, when her condo had been searched then emp-tied, if she shouldn't warn him anyway, in case they went after him as a means of getting to her.

The questions went round and round in her head until she wanted to cover her ears and scream. She had one other option—to stay on Martinique and try to find John herself. Oh, that would tick him off. The thought almost made her smile. But even if she some-how found out where they held him, what weapon did she have to force his release? A bunch of bananas and a razor-edged palm frond? More likely she'd walk right into some kind of trap, and then all hope would be lost.

It was getting dark. She rubbed one arm and then the other. Whatever she was going to do, she had to make a decision quick. She'd crouch behind this bush all night if she thought John would suddenly show up in the morning, but that was unlikely. She couldn't save him single-handedly, but neither could she leave him on the island, suffering God knew what fate.

Her options narrowed to one. She swore under her breath. She had to find a phone. Then she had to call her father.

Cali shifted on the hard plastic seat in the American consulate's office. Her entire body was sore and screaming in protest from thirty-six hours without sleep. She tried her best to ignore it. She tightened her grip on the backpack and kept her eyes trained on the door. It had taken her most of the night to get off the mountain in the most roundabout way possible. She'd skirted two small villages, finally stumbling into the slightly more developed burg of Aurignac. She'd waited out the rest of the night hiding behind the building of a small, independently owned car-rental business. That morning she'd used traveler's checks to rent a car. She'd weighed the risk of them being traced back to the company against using a bus. But she had no idea if such arrivals and departures were somehow being watched. When she discovered the rental place was so small that they filled out forms by hand and asked for a safety deposit up front, she opted for the car.

She'd made it into the capital city of Fort-de-France by midday and to the consulate's office less than fifteen minutes after that. It was the only thing she'd known to do. She'd wanted a phone that she could use and a place to sit where no one was likely to bother her. She had spent a little time wondering if whoever was behind this had someone planted in the local government, but she had to draw the line on paranoia at some point. So, there she sat, waiting.

The door suddenly swung open and a man ducked under the frame and entered the room. He'd had to duck a lot of door frames, she thought absently, knowing her jaw had dropped open, but too weary to care about appearing rude.

He was the biggest man she'd ever seen. It took considerable control not to leap out of her seat and make a run for it. But the only escape route was currently blocked by him.

"Cali Stanfield?"

She stared at him. He was actually quite handsome when you got past his enormous size. Well over six feet and she swore almost as wide at the shoulders, he was an amazing spectacle. His arms were the size of her thighs. His hands could likely crush her skull with little or no effort. The only thing that kept her from making a run for it anyway was the affable, little-boy smile on his face. She'd heard of eyes that twinkled before, but she'd never seen any until now. He had bright white teeth, dimples that somehow made him look innocent, and shaggy brown hair that fell immediately back on his forehead after he raked it away. He looked like a giant, overgrown kid. Harmless. Sort of.

She nodded. "T. J. Delahaye?"

"Live and in the considerable flesh."

He stepped forward and extended a hand the size of a small ham toward her. She half expected the floor to rumble under his weight, but he moved gracefully, with almost total silence. She was intimidated and oddly reassured at the same time. His callused hand engulfed hers but was surprisingly gentle. "You're one of McShane's team?" A man his size could *be* an entire team in his own right. Besides, who was going to tell him he couldn't play?

He nodded. "You were lucky. I had just checked in with Spook Central when your father tracked down McShane's work history. We've had a few shake-ups in management of late and we're a bit shorthanded."

"John told me."

T. J. studied her for several nerve-racking seconds, then said, "I see."

How in the world a man the size of a small mountain could pull off looking vulnerable, she had no idea. But discovering he was a man of surprising talents continued the process of reassuring her.

"Well, our temporary leader just filed a short list to expand the team. Until they are rounded up, I'm on leave." He smiled. Cali felt the tension flow from her. The man had a smile as wide as the Mississippi and just as unstoppable. "What better place to spend my first vacation in eight years than the Caribbean?"

The tension returned. "I'm sorry. Really. I had no idea where else to turn. If there's anyone else—"

"Hey, I'm here. I'm willing. Why not, huh?" His shrug was as casual as his smile.

She blamed lack of sleep for her reaction to his overly relaxed manner. "You seem awfully cavalier about this, considering one of your teammates is very probably fighting for his—" She broke off and looked away when her throat suddenly tightened. Her lapse in front of T. J. only served to increase her ire. She swung her head back toward him seconds later, not caring what he might hear in her voice. "Can you rescue him?"

"Won't be the first time." He stood in front of her, hands loosely tucked in the pockets of his pleated hiking shorts, one booted foot propped on its heel. His calves were roughly the size of Rhode Island, making her wonder, only half hysterically, if he stomped the enemy out.

"Ready whenever you are," she said, feeling anything but.

"Uh-uh. I work alone, Miss Stanfield."

She didn't bother to correct him on the name. "Well, I can't sit here waiting. I won't." She stood, still clutching the pack to her chest. "I don't want to interfere, but he's in this mess because of me."

"I'm sure he won't hold that against you."

His affable smile was beginning to grate on her nerves. She'd trade it for McShane's implacable mask in half a heartbeat. "I wouldn't be so sure about that. This isn't the first time I've caused him trouble." In fact, every contact she'd had with John McShane had usually involved her in hot water and him trying not to get boiled in the same pot. He'd been successful—until now. She noticed that her admission had sent T. J. on full alert. She immediately switched gears. "I won't get in your way, Mr. Delahaye."

"T. J.'ll do."

"Whatever," she said, less than graciously. Lack of sleep, stress overload, and digesting the gritty remains of one too many cups of coffee had worn her control down to a frazzle. "Listen, I meant that. I won't get in your way—"

"I know you won't, because I have you booked on a private flight to the States in"—he checked his watch—"less than one hour. Your father will meet you at the other end along with another teammate of mine. Our temporary leader, in fact. You really must rate. Scottie is a bit busy these days to play chauffeur, even for an ambassador's daughter."

So she wasn't to have even a moment's reprieve. Tension balled up even further inside her. She'd known all the ramifications of calling her father. But knowing them and dealing with the reality of them were two different things.

With renewed effort to win this fight, she said, "I'm part of this situation. Hell, I *am* this situation. I won't—can't—sit idly by while more people risk their lives on my behalf. I need to be involved." Her voice had risen and even she could hear the edge of hysteria in her demands.

T. J. laid a massive palm on her shoulder. The warmth of his hand was oddly reassuring. Still fuming, she at least stopped pacing.

"Trust me, you won't be idle. Scottie is already setting up a command station back home. You'll be putting in some long hard hours decoding that book and documenting the program your late husband wrote."

His voice was a deep low rumble that vibrated throughout her body, as strangely soothing as his touch was gentling. If she wasn't so preoccupied with the mess she was in, terrified at what was happening to John, she might have enjoyed talking with Agent Delahaye.

But even his overwhelming presence wasn't enough to change her focus. She shook her head. "We know what we have. Documenting this program won't keep whoever it is from coming after me."

"Yes, but this way we'll know exactly what kind of bait it is we're offering."

"Bait?" Cold dread crawled through her, making the nausea worsen.

Still smiling, T. J. nodded almost happily. "Yep. Best way to find out who wants this so badly. Trap 'em, grill 'em, book 'em. End of problem."

Cali straightened, stepping away from the natural shelter of T. J.'s towering body. "I'll go back. I'll work on the program."

His smile spread to a grin. There was actually relief in his eyes. "Great. Let's hit it." Not wasting any time, he turned to the door. "Stay right behind—"

"On one condition."

He turned slowly back to her, his expression wary rather than relieved. "Namely?"

"I deliver the bait."

EIGHT

"Tell me you didn't agree." Speaking cost him. John swallowed a groan. Groaning hurt. It was a toss-up which throbbed worse, his face or his torso. But nothing short of death—which, if not for a certain blonde, he'd have wished for a hundred times over in the last two days—was going to keep him from grilling, and perhaps killing, his teammate.

"I didn't see as I had much choice, McShane. Your lady is champion material in the stubborn and bullheaded division." T. J. handed him another ice pack. "I can see why you two hit it off."

John stared out the dusty window of the small airless truck he'd been bounced around and holed up in for the last hour. "She's not my anything. Which is moot since I plan on killing her as soon as I get done with you."

T. J.'s chuckle would have earned him a good

right hook, if, at the moment, John had had a good right anything to deliver it with.

"How much farther to the damn plane? This island can't be that big."

"Five minutes. We're taking the roundabout route. I don't expect a thank-you or anything for saving your sorry hide." He paused. "What's left of it. You're lucky I found you when I did, partner."

"How'd you manage that anyway? Ask directions at the corner gas station?"

"Well, dragging your carcass through the brush left a nice wide trail for me to follow. They got a little cleaner after that, but there aren't too many places to hide on this island. You know you could have helped me out a little."

"Sorry, I was too unconscious to leave a trail of bread crumbs."

"You woke up at some point."

John massaged his ribs, hoping they were only bruised. "Yeah, hell of an alarm clock they use."

"And you know we're a little short of help right now. I couldn't throw together a complete chase team."

"Hell, Delahaye, you *are* a chase team." He winced. Talking hurt. "I always wondered how a man your size moved so quietly. Even I didn't hear you."

T. J. shot him a wide grin. "Spy boots."

John almost snorted, would have if he wasn't reasonably certain he'd rip something open.

"You could have helped me out by getting a visual of at least one of your genial hosts."

"Gee, I'm sorry, Delahaye. Must have been all the blood in my eyes at the time." John tried like hell to curb his tongue and his temper. It wasn't like him to let anything, even the beating of a lifetime, get to him.

T. J.'s "super-spy stuff is my life" attitude was the one John normally adopted during an assignment. Hell, it was how he normally really felt. His credo had been "If you gotta go, take the bad guys with you." When you truly didn't care if you lived or died, it wasn't hard to be nonchalant about your work.

But now he did care if he lived. Or if he died.

"There were two of them. Neither one had any rank. Warm-ups for whoever was coming in after they loosened my mouth up a bit. They kept a hood on me while we 'talked.' Otherwise I was kept in that room you found me in. I take it you waited for them to step out?"

"Maybe they were out picking up Mr. Big himself, but yes, you were alone." T. J. clucked his tongue. "Should know better than to leave their baby-sitting charge alone. Never know what trouble they can get into." His smile faded. "I wish I'd had the manpower to send someone after them."

John was silent for a moment. He didn't bother to mention that T. J. could have gone after the two goons and left him behind for later retrieval. In T. J.'s place, John would have done the same thing.

A small moan escaped him when T. J. hit a ditch. The moan made him wince. His mouth was more swollen tissue than functioning muscle at the moment. He didn't have to brave it out in front of his teammate, but survival instincts didn't kick in and back out that easily. Using much of whatever control he had left, he clamped down on the surge of pain and the resulting roll of nausea, and shifted to look at the man who had just single-handedly pulled him out of hell. "Thanks, T."

T. J. glanced at him, held his gaze for a split second longer, then turned back to the road. "That green color looks good with all the red, black, and blue. It'll be downright pretty when the yellow and purple kick in."

John didn't respond. He kept his gaze on his still-smiling teammate for another silent moment, then finally looked away. Ah, hell. T. J. knew. John had been compromised.

It wasn't anything simple, or easily understood, like caving in to torture. His fall from grace resulted from something far more destructive and dangerous.

He'd been made vulnerable. His team knew it. But far worse, the enemy knew it. He'd been rendered useless. A liability was all he'd be now.

The very idea should have devastated him. His whole life had just been gutted like nothing more than the sputtering flame of a spent candle. Commitment to the team was all he'd had. Others had taken the time to cultivate at least a minimal private life between assignments, solo though their ventures were by necessity. Not John McShane. He thrived on his job. In fact, he'd taken on and successfully accomplished more missions than anyone else in the history of the Dirty Dozen. No one questioned his dedication. Nor did they understand his motives. No one had ever asked. Other than the original team leader, Seve Delgado, no one ever would. They'd each been handpicked by Del and that was enough.

They all had their reasons, and personal revelation was not necessary for them to work well as a cohesive unit. In fact, it was their unique ability to be completely insular that enabled them to work well together. They weren't even vulnerable to each other. The perfect agent. The perfect team. And John McShane had been the best of the lot.

Until now. Now he was flawed. Fatally so.

Sore and raw in more places than he wasn't, facing a life that held nothing, he could think of only one thing: Cali.

She'd survived. She'd saved his life. T. J. hadn't said how she'd tracked him down, leaving that for her to explain if she chose to. She instilled loyalty very easily, it seemed. But he had a pretty good idea of what she'd done. This mission had Ambassador Stanfield's fingerprints all over it. He wasn't sure how he felt about that, or the sacrifice Cali had made by making that move. But by placing the call, she'd very likely saved herself as well. He'd do what he could to extricate her from Stanfield's very long reach as soon as he could. Right after he made damn sure she gave up the idiotic idea of using herself as bait.

It was the least he could do for her. It was also all he could do for her. The team would handle matters now. From here on out, his role in this mission had ended, just as his role on the team had ended. It hit him that for the first time in his entire life he had no idea what his role was.

As T. J. pulled the truck onto a private airstrip where a small Cessna waited, John realized that what made him feel truly lost was that, for the second time in his life, he was going to have to walk out on Cali.

Cali heard the commotion in the living room and paused in her work. She took an absent sip of cold coffee, her staff of life for the past three days, and stared at the computer screen, largely ignoring the intrusion as she mentally ran through several complex calculations. It was T. J.'s rumbling bass that brought her to full alert. Scottie Giardi's throaty but fully female voice followed.

Cali was out of the chair and to the door of her office—located on the second-floor bedroom of a small town house tucked away in a nondescript suburb in northern Virginia—in a heartbeat. No one would tell her anything about John, other than that T. J.'s mission had been successful. She'd all but begged her dad, Ms. Giardi, and both of the other men who had temporarily protected her, for information.

A rough, halting voice stopped her dead halfway down the staircase. McShane. And from the sounds of the discussion, he wasn't too happy. She didn't know whether to race down the stairs or to run back and hide in her office. She was compelled to do both. Her need to see for herself how he'd fared won out.

The conversation ceased when she hit the mid-point landing. Her head and heart had been racing too fast for her to make out the actual discussion, but she grasped the gist. McShane wanted her off the case after she'd cracked the rest of the virus program.

She paused to gather her control. From her position on the steep staircase, she could see three sets of feet. All of a sudden she wasn't sure she wanted to see John. No one had said anything. But she sensed, knew, that he hadn't fared well. He'd been held hostage for two days.

All toes shifted toward her.

"Cali? Come on down. Someone here wants to talk to you." Scottie didn't bother to disguise her sarcasm.

Time was up. *This is what you wanted, right? A chance to see him one more time? To make sure he was okay. To tell him you were sorry for dragging him into your life again. Thank him.*

Tell him good-bye.

Cali took two steps down. Beat-up hiking boots took two steps forward. John McShane came slowly into view. She took her time looking up. His legs looked fine. He hadn't limped. At least not that she could tell. He wore a loose navy-and-white-striped polo shirt, untucked. She wondered what type of gun was hidden underneath. His arms were tanned, but before she could scan them for bruises or cuts, she made the mistake of looking up. She gasped despite her promise to herself not to react.

John's steely gaze betrayed none of his pain. His beautiful face was multihued, swollen, cut, and stitched. His arms, when she forced her gaze away, were also lined with bruises and more than a few cuts and scrapes. The rest of his body didn't bear thinking about. The details assaulted her mind anyway.

She looked back at his face, into his eyes. Her own were glassy. If T. J. and Scottie were still in the room, she was totally unaware of them. "I am so sorry." Her voice was shaky and any second her eyes would brim over. Both things angered her; control was a prime asset these days and one she hoarded like a bandit.

But if she was angry at her body's not-so-subtle signs, she was furious at what had been done to John. "I should have never sent you that note."

"I'm a big boy, Cali. I knew what I was getting into."

His voice was tight, restrained. Because of the pain? Or was it anger?

She stepped down again, one step from the landing, bringing them eye to eye. Less than a foot of space separated them. "I still feel responsible." Her fingers twitched with the need to reach up and touch him, to caress his bumps and bruises, to check for herself that his pulse still ran strong, that his skin was still warm. Her gaze drifted helplessly to his half-swollen mouth. She longed to find out if he still tasted the same.

Wrong path, Cali. You're supposed to be saying good-bye.

"Well, don't be. I'm not usually so sloppy." A snicker snapped at their attention. Cali caught John wincing as he turned his head toward T. J. "The peanut gallery is excused."

"Now, isn't that gratitude for you? Save a guy's bacon, and all you get is—"

"A raise," Scottie cut in. She grabbed T. J.'s arm and pulled. "Which will turn into a penalty if you don't follow me into the kitchen." She pulled hard, but it was like trying to move a mountain. He didn't budge.

"Aw, come on, boss, it was just getting interest—"

"Now, Special Agent Delahaye." She dropped his arm and lifted one beautifully shaped eyebrow instead.

"Yes, ma'am."

If Cali hadn't been more preoccupied with John, she'd have laughed at the picture made by the hulking T. J. all but pouting as he dutifully followed his boss from the room. A smile curved her mouth anyway, when he turned at the door and shot her a wink, a thumbs-up, and mouthed, Give em hell, Cali.

She winked back, but sobered instantly when she turned to John and found him studying her intently.

"I didn't know what else to do," she said, her voice soft but not with apology. "I'd do it again,

McShane." She kept her eyes on his and away from his swollen mouth and bruised jaw. Visions of what his body must look like assaulted her no matter how she tried to squelch them.

"You did the right thing. You saved both our lives—and the program."

"Did they find out—"

"Not from me."

"I never doubted that. That's why I called my father. It wasn't right, what was happening to you." She looked away, paced past him to the coffee table then back again. She stopped in front of him, hands clenched at her sides to keep from touching him, caressing his bruises. As if that would make it all better. The only thing that would make McShane better would be her staying out of his life. Permanently.

"I couldn't stand it." Her admission was barely a rough whisper. She hadn't meant to say it, not with such raw emotion. But she'd looked back at his beautiful battered face and there was no hope for it. She reached up but curled her fingers inward just shy of touching his cheek. His hand snagged hers before she could drop it to her side. She felt more than saw him flinch and tried to pull away, not wanting to cause him any more pain than he was already feeling. He held tight. Not knowing which was worse, she stopped fighting with him, just as she admitted that his warm, rough hand felt good wrapped around hers.

She had a house full of highly trained professionals, not to mention the oppressive shadow of her father, focused exclusively on keeping her—and Nathan's program—safe. Yet it was the touch of a battered, beaten man that made her feel safe.

He pulled her palm to his face. She felt his ragged breath in the uneven vibration of his skin under her fingertips. She tried to cup her hand so as not to hurt him, but he pressed her hand more firmly to his cheek. His steely gaze locked on hers. "I wouldn't betray you, Cali."

Was there more than determination in his eyes? Did she dare search for the answer? "That's what worried me."

"I'm okay. You called in the good guys. They'll get the job done."

"*We'll* get the job done."

He dropped her hand. If there had been anything like concern or . . . other things she didn't dare consider in his expression, it was gone now. Now there was only cold determination. This was Special Agent McShane she was dealing with.

"You work on decrypting the program, let the team handle the rest."

"I can't do that."

"Don't be stupid, Cali. You don't have to put yourself in the line of fire. That's what we're paid to do, and we do it very well."

"Yeah, I can see that." She regretted the snapped-off words the instant they were out of her mouth. What made it ten times worse was the flash of emotion that briefly lit John's eyes. "That was inexcusable. I'm sorry. I didn't mean it. It's just—"

"Do you have any idea how worried I was about you?"

The intensity in his quietly spoken words made her stomach clutch. "Worried? About me?"

"Yes. About you." He stepped closer. Even black-and-blue and with a slight limp she detected now, she could still feel the harnessed energy that seemed to radiate from him. The idea of having that energy and intensity focused on her . . .

She swallowed against the sudden tight ball lodged in her throat. Her stomach felt queasy. Her temples throbbed. At no time had this ever felt like a game to her. But for some reason the idea of him worrying about her while other men were beating him . . . It was too real. Too horrific. Too much.

"Then I'm doubly sorry. I should never have called you into this."

"Why in hell not? You have other friends who do this sort of thing?" His attempt at humor was ruined by the continued hard edge in his tone.

"Friends don't ask friends to risk their lives. And we were hardly even that. We haven't so much as swapped Christmas cards in ten years."

"You did the right thing, Cali. It's not as if you could have looked in the Yellow Pages. You already told me the local police were of no help, and it was going to the feds that got you into this mess in the first place."

Her smile was hollow. "You stand there, more blue skin than tan, hurting in more places than you don't, because you did a favor for me, and you're trying to convince me I did the right thing." She shook her head, her grin more real. "I don't know which one of us is crazier."

"It's no longer you against the world. The team will handle it. Scottie had no problem getting an okay for this."

"I can't imagine Scottie having much of a problem getting anything she wants." Cali had been impressed and just a tiny bit jealous of the woman sitting in the kitchen. John's current boss was no small, frail thing. She was taller than John, broad-shouldered in the way swimmers were, but with a waist and rounded hips that gave her just enough curve to make her more knockout than Amazon. She had long hair, the rich shade of mahogany, that she wore combed straight off her face, making her average features somehow appear exotic. She was quick to smile and had a razor-sharp wit aimed at herself more often than others. It was totally impossible not to like her. She was the only woman Cali had met who could make jeans and a tweed blazer look like a power suit. The woman had presence in spades. Even if Scottie hadn't earned her respect and admiration with the efficient yet compassionate way she'd handled all aspects of Cali's problem, the fact that she'd moved T. J. when the man clearly hadn't wanted to be moved was enough to put the woman high on Cali's list for life.

"Yeah, she's one of the best. Del made a smarter move than even he knew naming her interim team leader." There was no mistaking John's sincerity.

The twinge of jealousy returned. Only this time it had nothing to do with Scottie's job performance. "I'm sure he did," she said evenly. "But that doesn't mean I'm going to sit here and—"

"You're not just sitting here!"

Cali jumped at John's sharp tone. She also didn't miss the way he tightened up, as if bracing against the pain. "If we're going to argue, why don't we sit over here and do it." She walked to the couch. "It's hurting me to watch you stand there."

She sat down. John stayed where he was. "It's killing me to think of you placing yourself in danger again."

Cali opened her mouth, then closed it. There was no doubting the sincerity in these words either.

He moved closer. He didn't let it show—a rule that was probably in the super-secret-agent training book—but she knew his evenly paced steps cost him. Her muscles tightened against the urge to reach out and help him as he lowered himself onto the couch next to her. About the very last thing he needed right now was help from her.

The irony of that sentiment, considering their current disagreement, wasn't lost on her. But no matter how deep and conflicting the emotions he aroused in her, she was not backing down.

"I don't want you to worry about me. That's not in your job description."

"I've told myself that for ten years. It doesn't seem to make a difference."

Again he'd shocked her into silence. *Ten years?* "I shouldn't have called you then either. A man like you, with your sense of obligation . . ." An obligation he'd obviously never let go of. His loyalty to Nathan ran as deep as his loyalty to his job. Nathan had been the same way. She should have known. "But I had nowhere else to turn," she whispered, more to herself than to him.

He laid his hand on hers. She didn't pull away.

"You didn't this time either," he said.

She felt the pull of his eyes on her, let it build up, until she had no choice but to look up.

"I didn't mean for you to feel obligated to me. Because of Nathan—"

"That's not why I worried about you, Cali. My partnership with Nathan is not why I flew halfway around the world to find you."

"Then why . . . ?" She shook her head and looked away. "You don't have to tell me. You came. You helped me. Again. You probably shouldn't have." She looked back at him. "But I'm glad you did. And not just for the program. I shouldn't say this, not with everything else, but . . ."

Common sense kicked in at the last moment and she trailed off. Some things definitely were better left unsaid. The warm feel of his fingertips on her chin caught her off guard.

He stared at her in silence until the tension between them was snapping sharp. "Yeah," he said finally, a touch of resignation in his voice. "I know what you mean." He dropped his hand back to hers again, only this time he picked it up. He examined her palm, then the back of her hand, tracing her veins and the length of each finger with the interest and focus of a surgeon. "There are many things I've wanted to say to you for years and knew I shouldn't. So I didn't. I got as far away from you as I could to keep from saying them."

There was no mistaking the not-quite-hidden need in his voice, or the matching look in his eyes. He'd reached some sort of wall. The problem was she didn't know whether he wanted her to encourage him to go over it, or keep him safely on his side.

There was a sudden surge of noise from the lower level, where Scottie had set up a command center of sorts. Both agents appeared from the kitchen and made a beeline for the stairs, with T. J. tossing out a brief, "Pardon us," before disappearing behind Scottie.

She looked back to John. "You need to go down there too?" She had no idea what she'd expected, but it had not been the flash of bleak resignation that crossed his face before he masked it. Also masked was any trace of the vulnerability she'd spied only moments earlier. He rubbed his fingers over her hand, his attention obviously elsewhere, then abruptly stopped the soothing motion, dropping her hand as if just realizing he was touching her. He shifted away.

"Go," she urged, thinking it would help them both to return to their respective corners. "This was getting us nowhere." Liar. She had no idea where their conversation had been taking them, but it had definitely been somewhere. Somewhere she probably had no business going. Unable to shake the hollow feeling that accompanied that thought, she pushed to a stand.

"I'd better get back to work anyway." She gestured to the floor above them.

"You're not going down?"

"If it affects this case, I'm sure I'll hear about it at some point." She wondered at the set look on his face. "Don't think about locking me out of this, McShane. I'm in to the end. It's my problem."

"It's the country's problem. You don't have to risk your life beyond this point, Cali. You do what you do best. Work out the program. Without that, we have nothing to bait them with. We don't need you as human bait. Leave that part to the trained professionals."

She didn't want to argue with him. She was dying to know what he'd meant by his earlier statement. What had he spent ten years running from? Why had he been compelled to run from her at all? *Dangerous questions, Cali Ellis.* "Why don't you head on down there. I'm sure that, whatever the situation, Scottie and T. J. would appreciate your presence in command central."

"No."

"Fine. Maybe it's better for you to rest anyway. Can I get you anything before I head back upstairs?" As if she was really going to be able to concentrate with McShane anywhere on the premises and with all that unfinished business between them. "Something to drink?"

"No, thank you."

"All right." She turned toward the stairs, then paused at the base. Something wasn't right. "You okay?"

"Define *okay*."

One hand resting on the newel post, she turned back to face him. "Is something else going on here that I don't know about? You want me to call Scottie or T. J. up here?"

"I can't block your involvement in this case, Cali."

Surprised, she said, "But you just spent the last fifteen minutes trying to talk me out of it."

"I said *can't*. I want to. If there was any way I could, I would."

"I'm sure you could find a way to pull strings. But I appreciate you letting me do what I need to do."

"I don't want you hurt."

How did he look so indomitable sitting on the couch, one foot propped on the coffee table, his body all banged up, his eyes so hollow? Hollow. "I don't want you hurt either," she said. "But that's why I have to do this. Don't you see, I can't stand the thought of anyone else getting hurt. Or worse." She couldn't stifle the shudder. "It's already cost too much. Nathan. You."

"I'm okay."

She stepped closer to him. "No, you're not. And I'm not talking about the obvious." He looked worse than beaten, he looked . . . lost. "What's going on, McShane? Why can't you do whatever you please with your team?"

"Because as of nine o'clock this morning, I'm no longer officially on the team. That's why."

NINE

"What?" Cali crossed to the couch, stopping next to his outstretched leg, hands on her hips. "That doesn't make any sense! It wasn't your fault you were caught. You saved my life." She swung around. "I'll talk to Scottie."

"I wasn't removed. I resigned."

She whirled back. Her face gradually lost color.

John asked himself for the dozenth time in the last five minutes what in the hell he was doing there. He'd known going in that he had next to no chance of getting her to change her mind about using herself as delivery woman. But he'd come anyway.

"It's my fault. You're leaving your job because of me."

Yes, he was. "It's not your fault."

"You left the Blue Circle right after helping me. Now you're leaving again. What am I supposed to think?"

Good question, McShane. What are you going to tell her? I'm leaving because I love you? Because I need you when I've never needed anyone?

He'd resigned. Technically, and for the first time in fifteen years, he was a free agent—in every way. He had choices.

He rubbed a hand over his face. He'd been sure of the choices he'd made that morning. But now that he was with Cali, things weren't so clear-cut any longer. He realized now they never had been. Ah, hell.

"You're supposed to think I know what I'm doing." Though why she should when he didn't have a clue was beyond him. He massaged his temples. "You're supposed to think that any decisions I made were in the best interest of the team." It didn't help. There was no hiding from her. Ten years should have taught him that. He dropped his hand and looked at her. "In the best interest of you."

Her eyes lit on fire. "So that's why you're here? To make sure the team and I do what John McShane thinks is best for us?"

He sighed heavily. He shouldn't have come. He should have had T. J. or Scottie find a way to cut her out of the deal. He should have found some other way to keep her safe, some other way to say good-bye.

"Cali . . ." He had no idea what to say.

She stepped closer, sat on the coffee table so she was eye level with him. He couldn't look away.

You can't run away either, his little voice warned. *Not this time.*

"What about what's best for you? What does John

McShane want?" She huffed out a breath, swore softly, raked a hand through her already thoroughly mussed hair. He saw the fatigue etched around her eyes. Saw that he was adding to it.

"Never mind," she said quietly. "I have no right. Your life is yours."

She stood. John thought he'd hated pain on her face. He hated the resignation more.

Did you expect her to beg you to stay?

The hell of it was, he had no idea what he expected. Then or now.

"However, you no longer have a right to tell me what to do with my life either." The words were flatly stated. Cool. Her eyes were none of those things. She stepped back. The distance was far more emotional than physical. He felt both keenly.

He was doing the right thing, he told himself silently. Free agent or not, he had nothing to offer her. Except a past he couldn't change. And a future he couldn't predict.

"I'm almost done decrypting the program." She crossed her arms, studied the backs of her hands as she continued. "I don't know how long it will take to analyze what Nathan did, determine how dangerous the completed work was or how close he was to finishing it. But I do know that I'm the best one—the only one—to lure the other side in and keep their suspicions to a minimum." Her increasingly strident tone gentled as he continued to stare at her in silence. "Don't worry about me."

"Sure." He didn't rein in the harshness. What difference did it make now? "No problem. Out of sight, out of mind."

His sarcasm surprised her. Her eyes narrowed. "You know your team. They'll work out all the logistics."

"Is that what Scottie told you? T. J.? Do you have any idea what little problem you've created? Do you realize that three of the four team members that existed when you contacted me are in this town house? That Scottie is in the middle of several other assignments, not to mention rebuilding a team that can't sustain any further losses?"

"Then how in good conscience can you leave them now?"

"I had no choice. I'm compromised. More liability than help. We've taken too many of these hits. I'd only hurt the team worse down the line. It's not worth the risk."

"You mean because the other side saw you? They don't know who you work for."

"Who told you that?"

She leveled him with a flat look. "No one had to tell me that." While he was busy being rocked by that dead-on, unequivocal appraisal, she went on. "So work behind the scenes until this is over. Head up a new assignment elsewhere."

"It's not that simple. The risk goes beyond this case."

She threw up her hands, turned, and paced to the front door. She put her hand on the knob then turned to face him. "Then what in the hell are you doing here? You're all worried about the risk you represent to us. You've decided you're unable to function as an agent. Well then, you'd better leave, since you can no longer associate yourself with this team."

John couldn't clamp down on the groan as he heaved himself off the couch. She turned the knob.

"Don't." He flattened his palm on the door, smacking it back shut. His face was dangerously close to hers. He pushed it closer. Her expression was defiant, mutinous.

Beautiful.

"I don't take orders from you." She kept her hand on the knob. "If you came here on the noble mission to save me once again from myself, then you can leave. I heard what you have to say."

"You heard, but you didn't listen."

She shrugged. "You win some, you lose some. You can't bully people into doing what you want all of the time."

"You have no idea what I want, Cali Ellis." He felt his control careen wildly to the point of no return.

"You claim to love your work. Yet you're leaving it. You say you're loyal to your team, yet you're leaving them. You claim to care what happens to me, yet you're leaving me too. I don't think you know what you want, McShane."

He tugged her hand off the doorknob and pressed it to his chest. "Feel that?" He could feel the thumping beat himself, could hear it drumming inside his ears.

She opened her mouth, but before she could

speak, he yanked her hand up, pressed her fingers to his temple. "I know what I want." He tapped her hand. "In here, I know what's best. For you. For the team. And, by default, for me."

He tugged her hand back to his chest. "But in here I'm lost. I have no guidelines for following what I feel. As a rule, I try not to feel anything in here."

"Is that so wrong?" she asked, her voice a bare rasp. She pressed harder with her fingertips. "Since when is feeling wrong?" She flattened her palm.

"Since I took on a job where 'feeling' with your head keeps you alive and feeling with your heart gets you dead. And if you're lucky, you're the only one to die." He covered her hand, pressed it harder. "It has always been a fair trade for me. I like what I do. My work satisfies me. I'm good at thinking with my head."

"Then why are you leaving?"

He lowered his mouth. A whisper away from her lips, he said, "Because right now I can only think with my heart."

There was no anger in his kiss, Cali thought. No trace of the hard edge that lined his voice. His lips were warm, soft. Cali opened her lips under his, telling herself she only did so because she didn't want to hurt his swollen mouth. But she had no handy excuse for why she accepted his gentle entry willingly, why she didn't struggle when he pulled her hand to his shoulder and slid his around her waist, why she moved fluidly when he tugged her closer, or sighed at the way he fitted too perfectly against her. She told herself that it was fatigue mixed with confusion that made her eyes burn at the way her heart beat directly into his. That she really wasn't falling in love with John McShane.

How could she when they both knew this kiss was hello and good-bye in one unbearably sweet, heart-breaking package.

She shifted her mouth away when the burn threatened to edge over into real tears. She rested her forehead on his chin, telling herself she needed to get her bearings, regain her control, then she'd step out of his arms. And not think about how that magic circle was the only place she wanted to be. It was where she felt safe. At peace. Complete.

She'd secure her own safety. Make her own peace. Hadn't losing Nathan and the baby taught her about trusting in magic circles?

When she stepped away, felt his hands leave her, looked up into gray eyes that were no longer empty but still hollow, and knew exactly how that felt . . . that was when she asked herself how she would ever make herself complete. One half of a whole was how she felt.

One half had been good enough for ten years. It would be good enough again.

Somehow.

"McShane, come down here. Please." Scottie's husky contralto was more abrupt than usual.

John shifted between her and the door. "You going up to work?"

Other than a slight rasp to his already deep voice, nothing betrayed what he was thinking, feeling.

She nodded. That was her choice, right? Work. Risk her life but not her heart.

"McShane?" This time it was T. J., his voice booming up the stairwell.

John swore under his breath. "Right there." Then slid around her without touching. Cali ached at how such a tiny span of space could feel like a gaping chasm.

"Still answering to the call." Cali turned to lean back against the door and crossed her arms as he moved slowly to the top of the stairs.

"I want to talk to you again before I leave." He barely glanced at her.

Her heart hitched despite the fact that she'd told herself this was good-bye. *Tell him that*, her little voice said. She shrugged and pushed casually away from the door. "You know where to find me."

His eyes zeroed in on hers. "Yes. I do. Don't ever forget that, Cali."

For a beaten man, he disappeared down the stairs silently and swiftly, leaving her standing there open-mouthed, any hope for composure gone.

There would be no easy good-bye with John McShane.

As she trudged upstairs to her office her mind shifted to familiar patterns, spinning out probabilities versus possibilities, figuring angles, calculating risk factors, juggling theories with fact.

The only problem was she wasn't thinking about

Nathan's program. She was thinking about John McShane.

John was beyond weary. His fatigue was cell-deep. Teetering much too close to the brink of physical and emotional exhaustion, he paused at the base of the stairs. It took less than fifteen seconds to determine that his usual mind-emptying routine wasn't going to work. Mainly because he realized that the only thing he'd ever had to clear out of it had been work-related in the first place.

He also realized exactly why Delgado had been so adamant about his agents having absolutely no emotional commitment outside the team. It went far deeper than being compromised if an enemy determined the weakness and used it directly against a team member. He'd seen the result of that, had lost another partner because of it.

Of course, Diego Santerra hadn't died. He'd left the team and gotten married. He'd asked John to be his best man.

"I'm best at only one thing." John remembered laughing. "And it isn't weddings."

Diego had understood, hadn't pushed. And John hadn't felt guilty about turning him down. He'd been closer to Diego than to anyone else on the team, but that was a relative thing. Diego was as insular as he was. Whereas John did his job because he was good at it, Santerra fought demons over his. John had been humbled by the request, but neither man was surprised by the intentionally light refusal. Vulnerability didn't only come in a package marked *opposite sex*. It was one of the reasons that Dirty Dozen members even shied away from personal involvement with each other outside the job. And that included standing up at a wedding.

John had been truly happy for Santerra. The man was more centered . . . settled, than he'd ever seen him. He was at peace. John remembered feeling a bit smug at the time, glad that his life was totally under control, his to command. He was at peace because no one owned him and he owed no one.

Two weeks later Cali's note had arrived.

He thought about how she'd felt in his arms. How she'd tasted under his mouth. How she'd matched his withdrawal, understood the why of it, knowing as he did that nothing good would come out of pursuing what had almost happened. Their lives had intertwined more than once, but not in the way that would form the basis for any kind of real relationship.

He should be grateful to Scottie and T. J. for calling him away, saving him from himself. Saving Cali from him.

The only thing he had left to do was make sure Cali was safe—safe to go back to her own life, to make her own choices, to find what would make her happy. To make her own peace.

But damn it all to hell, he could no longer deny that he wanted to be the cause of her happiness. He already knew he'd felt a peace in her arms he'd never known was possible.

He swore under his breath. He could never return that blessing. He was a man who'd been tangled up in the worst parts of her life, when all he'd ever wanted for her was the best.

"Hey, you ever gonna let her—" T. J. almost mowed John down. A wide grin split his face as he clapped John gently on his good shoulder and urged him down the hall. "Thought for a minute there I was gonna have to rescue you again. Or Cali. Wasn't sure if all that steam was coming from her ears or your eyes."

John scowled. "Your job is to walk into hell on a regular basis, Delahaye. Why are you always grinning like a damn fool?"

It had been a rhetorical question but one the large man answered cheerfully. "It's a proven fact that if you enjoy what you do, it reduces your stress. You'll live longer. And hey, like you said, our job can be murder. I can use all the help I can get."

"I'll help you," he muttered. John wanted—needed—the soothing familiar pattern of verbal sparring without crossing any real personal line. The solating, self-contained shield that had always naturally surrounded him had eroded somewhere back on Martinique. He wanted his balance back.

He moved into the recently created command center. "Scottie, if I shoot T. J. how long will it take to replace him? I might even consider coming back on the squad if you okay one clean shot."

Scottie's attention remained focused on the blue screen perched on her desk. "I usually want to shoot him on a daily basis, McShane, but I've managed to restrain myself. So can you."

"Oh wonderful." T. J. planted his meaty hands on his hips. "I just love peer appreciation. What am I, the Rodney Dangerfield of the team all of a sudden?"

Scottie swiveled her chair away from her desk to face them. Her expression was as smooth and sober as her tone had been. But there was something else in her hazel eyes that both men picked up like radar. The room stilled in the instant it took her to turn the monitor toward them.

"As to your rejoining the team, McShane, name me your price. I have to have you back. Immediately."

John stepped closer and looked at the screen. T. J. was breathing down his neck. They both swore at the same time.

"How in the hell did that happen?" T. J. asked, all teasing gone from his voice. He may have had more than a healthy exuberance about his work, but no one doubted his commitment was every bit as fierce.

"That's what I want to know." Scottie didn't have to explain to him or T. J. just how destructive the E-mail message on her screen truly was. The main threat was obvious. The message was clear. They wanted the program, all the notes, decrypted, all neat and tidy. Or they'd take Cali, in trade.

But it was much more insidious than that. They'd all been compromised. The note was personal, directed by name to all three of them. The sender's name, InnerCircle, meant nothing. But there was no doubt who'd sent it.

"Looks like there is more than a passing link to the old Blue Circle group." She lowered her head and swore, then looked to both of them. "This is us, guys," she said with more than a trace of disgust. "These guys are feds."

"They may have started as us, Scottie, but they aren't us now." T. J. paced the room, his long stride eating up the short space in several steps. "And I don't care who they are or what they're connected to. How in the hell do they plan to make good on that threat?" T. J. all but scoffed. "If they know who we are, know we have the program, then they know we have Cali."

"Cocky sons-of-bitches," Scottie agreed.

John heard them but wasn't listening. Tiny muscles in his jaw were twitching uncontrollably. He was disturbed on levels he hadn't known he'd possessed. He reread the note. Twice.

"Yeah, well, they haven't seen cocky." T. J. straightened. "Bring it on, baby. Bring it on."

Scottie pushed her fingers through her hair, revealing an unusual display of nerves. "I haven't got time for this." She spun back to the computer. "And they know that, dammit."

"I'll take care of them." John's voice was low and deceptively cool and brought complete silence to the room. He looked to T. J. "You take care of Cali."

"Don't you have that backward, pal?"

As the silence spun out, Scottie lifted questioning eyes to his. "We're all compromised, John. It's no different for us than it is for you now. T. J.'s better

equipped to go after them. I want you to take care of
Ms. Ellis. Get her out of here. I'll work on finding out
how they got on the inside, how they found us."

Grinning, T. J. stood next to John. "I knew you
couldn't leave us."

John didn't respond as he held Scottie's gaze. "I
can't do that."

Even T. J. stopped smiling.

John hadn't explained the full extent of his reasons
for resigning, and Scottie had taken him at his word.
He didn't know his teammate and temporary leader
all that well, knew her more by team reputation than
from sharing any sustained field experience with her.
But since she was a woman, he'd assumed—hoped, he
realized now—that she'd intuited the deeper reasons
for his defection.

Scottie whipped her gaze to John's, revealing the
fire that fed the steady, nerveless temperament that
had led to her being chosen temporary leader when
Diego Santerra had declined. John knew that he
wasn't alone in expecting her to remain leader. She'd
made it clear she considered it temporary, even
though the remaining members felt she was perfect
for the job.

"You *can* do it," she stated flatly. "Or we can't do
our jobs. You may not want yours any longer,
McShane, but the fact is, as much as it galls me to
admit it, if we don't round these guys up, ship them
off, and plug up the leak, then we may all be out of a
job."

No one mentioned that there were more than jobs

on the line. "I appreciate that." His gaze was just as steady, his tone just as cool. "I'm here, I'll do my part. But I can't be responsible for watching Cali."

"McShane—"

"John, I can watch her," T. J. broke in, his booming voice unusually soft. He was careful not to look at the temporary commander whose authority he'd overstepped. "But you know we'd have a better chance at success if I go in. We can't pull Blackstone in on this. He's holding down a two-man mission as it is."

John didn't need to be reminded of how thinly stretched the team was, or that he'd have likely been that second man. He'd picked through that minefield of guilt before turning in his resignation, had been grateful that none of his teammates had castigated him for his poorly timed decision.

He simply didn't see where he had any other options. He assumed they understood he wouldn't have made it otherwise. "We don't need Blackstone. Just do it my way and it will work out. Trust me."

Scottie stood up, stepped between the two men. "John, I'm not comfortable with having rank, much less pulling it, but Delgado left me in charge, and I take that responsibility seriously. Your strategic-planning history is nearly legendary. You could hide the President of the United States in the White House. Unless you give me a good reason, I can't see sending you in on roundup duty when I know damn well you're Ms. Ellis's best chance at survival." She waited him out.

He'd accepted his reasons, dealt with them. But thinking it was one thing. Saying it out loud was another commitment altogether. If he was ever to admit that he loved Cali Ellis, then the one he should first admit it to was the woman herself.

Scottie's patience wore visibly thin. "Well, McShane?"

"I've been compromised beyond discovery by the opposing team. I'm no longer the best man for that job."

"Which is fine by me," a fourth voice piped in. "I thought I'd made it clear that I don't want you or any of your team hiding me away."

Three heads turned. Cali stood at the base of the stairs, arms folded.

She spoke to everyone in the room, but her gaze was leveled directly at John. "I figured out what the Martinique connection is." She held out a copy of the snapshot she'd sent to him with her original plea for help.

John walked over and took the photo from her. "What are you talking about?"

"Adrian. He took the picture."

"Eudora's son."

Cali nodded. "It explains everything. It explains why Eudora was the messenger."

John studied the photo, then handed it back to her. "I know we talked about his coincidental departure from the island, but what does this prove?"

She took the picture, then stepped back. John fought the urge to drag her closer.

"It's the only other thing about the photo I hadn't thought of, analyzed. I've racked my brains on this. I kept trying to think of anything we might have talked about that day or about anything special that might have been captured on film, like a hiding place or something."

"What made you think of it now?"

For the first time her gaze faltered a bit. "I, uh, hit a tough spot upstairs and . . . and found myself staring at it." She took a breath and squared her shoulders. "It never occurred to me to think about who took the photo."

"How well did Nathan get to know him when you were there?"

"That's just it, as soon as I put it together, it all fell into place. Adrian was sort of a low-grade computer buff. The technology was brand-new back then but he had access to an 8088 and—" Cali broke off, her eyes wide with sudden excitement. She grabbed John's arm. "He owned an old computer! With a five-and-a-quarter disk drive."

As if she'd just realized the connection, she dropped his arm abruptly and backed away another half step. He wanted to tell her she couldn't run far enough away from him, that if he wanted to touch her, he would. On the heels of that thought came a more painful one. He wondered if he'd ever touch her—really touch her—again.

"His family actually owns some other property on other islands, and he'd decided to keep track—"

Her words brought him abruptly back to the topic

at hand. "They own land on other islands?" John swore under his breath. "Didn't you think that might be pertinent?"

"I'm sorry," she shot back, clearly frustrated with herself. "We never really talked about Adrian, and I didn't remember it until just now. It was ten years ago, John. I was on my honeymoon! I'm sorry if I wasn't paying close attention to everything going on around me, my focus was a bit narrow at the time."

John rubbed his palm down his face and blew out a quiet sigh. "Okay, okay. The question is, what exactly was his involvement then, and what is it now."

"If Adrian was contacted by someone in our government when this surfaced, then he's not a good guy."

"Doesn't look that way. But we still don't know for certain. Do you remember anything of what he and Nathan talked about?"

"Not really. He was just learning computers and was very excited about the technology. Nathan helped him set some stuff up on his system."

John swore. Loudly.

"What? What did I—" This time she broke off and swore. "He put some of this data on Adrian's hard drive."

John nodded. "Probably."

"But that was a decade ago, I doubt seriously Adrian still has that computer."

"Nathan didn't know it would be a decade. He was trying any way he knew how to safeguard his information. He figured Adrian wouldn't be at risk because he'd never find it, much less understand how to access it."

"But I would," Cali whispered. "Maybe Adrian found it on his hard drive at some point over the years. But he would have had no way of knowing where it had come from. He might have become more computer literate—"

"It's possible he was more than just a dumb geek-in-training, even then."

Cali frowned. "What do you mean?"

"Did you actually sit in on any of their conversations?"

"Well, of course I—" Then she thought about it. "Actually, come to think of it, he went down to Adrian's one afternoon when I had gone into town to pick up some things from Quéval. In fact, the picture was taken just before I left."

"Was that the only time they talked?"

She nodded. "For any length of time, yes. We ran into Adrian once or twice while we were there, but just to say hi." Cali fell silent, running it all through in her mind. She looked up at John. "You think he was Nathan's Blue Circle connection?"

"I don't think he was the man in charge of the program, but I do think he was the go-between, or one of them. If he owned that much real estate, then he was a good bet to recruit."

"Well, obviously Nathan didn't put anything on his computer that they didn't already have."

John nailed her with a steady look. "Or they had

information for ten years that they couldn't decrypt, and was therefore useless."

Cali swallowed. "So then I waltz in waving new information and ten-year-old bugs come crawling out of the woodwork."

Scottie stepped forward. "Good work, Cali."

Cali shifted her attention to the group's leader. "Thank you. I want to be in on the information exchange."

"No way."

Both women looked at John. Scottie spoke first. "I happen to agree with you on that."

"Super-spy or not, I'm part of this team. Without me, you'd have no contact name and no program. I gave you the name. You want the program, then use me to deliver it."

TEN

Cali scowled and crossed her arms. She'd tried to cross her legs several times, but the front seat of the small gray sports coupe wouldn't have accommodated a five-year old. She hadn't spoken one word to McShane in over four hours, since he'd bundled her into this death trap of a car "for her own good."

Proving he was as smart as his reputation, McShane hadn't spoken since then either. From the corner of her eye she could see his profile. She knew he was fuming. There was a measure of satisfaction in that, however small.

She watched as he shifted gears and took out his frustrations on the country road spinning out in front of them. They'd passed the "Welcome to North Carolina" sign some ways back. She didn't ask where they were headed. She could barely sit still with all the questions and furor churning inside her, but she would die before giving him the pleasure of telling her she was being kept in the dark about their destination "for her own good."

She ground her teeth and watched the sun begin to dip behind the mountains that loomed far ahead on the horizon. If the men who were after her could track her from California to Martinique to Virginia, she didn't understand where exactly there was left to hide. A sigh slipped out before she could stop it.

"Ah hell," John muttered under his breath.

An instant later she was forced to grab the dashboard when McShane suddenly swerved the car from the road, ducking down a narrow dirt track for another five yards, then all but yanking them to a stop behind a small stand of young pine trees. As soon as she got her bearings, she swung around, fearing she'd been so caught up in her silent indignation that she'd failed to notice a real threat. There was no one behind them.

She spun on him. "What in the hell is wrong with you? You could have flipped this toy box and killed us both."

He said nothing. He rested his wrists on the wheel, staring straight ahead as if he hadn't heard her. She couldn't help but stare at him. Seventy-two hours had elapsed since Scottie had used the authority of her position to override both John and Cali and set up the plan the way she thought best.

Cali had spent almost every one of those hours at the computer, fuming while she painstakingly crunched through each line of the rest of the program.

She put everything she had into decrypting what was left. It took every scrap of knowledge she'd gained in her career, along with a healthy dose of luck and faith. There had been hundreds of times she'd wanted to make a call, contact experts in her specialized field who could help her decipher the more challenging aspects of the code Nathan had developed. But with the team unable to pinpoint the source of the threat, there was to be no outside contact. They couldn't call in for additional help either.

She'd caught one break when, the day after they'd taken her to the town house, her father had been forced to return to his post in the Middle East when unrest had broken out there. She was grateful for the reprieve despite the reason for it. His assignments had always been in the globe's hot spots, so this was nothing new to her. And she knew that somehow he was being kept posted on every move she made, just as she knew that she'd have to deal with him about all of this sooner or later. Later was fine with her.

Right now they needed to figure out exactly what they had in their possession so the team could better determine who would benefit from the knowledge most. Of course, considering what the virus program could do—the potential for wreaking havoc on the economics of the nations of the world was mind-boggling—it didn't narrow the field much. Whoever wanted it would have to have the tools and resources to spread the virus on a massive scale. They needed to understand the virus program forward and back, inside and out.

Which was about how she'd felt, going two ways at once, when she'd been hustled straight from the computer into the car.

But she'd done it. She'd broken Nathan's code. It was all there, a complete program.

She'd asked herself one too many times during the last several hours what Nathan had been thinking even to develop such a thing. She was certain his reasons had to have been sound, but in the end, she'd had to back away from that debate all together. He was dead, so wondering why he'd done what he did brought only painful questions that would never be answered.

She shut down these thoughts and focused on her driver. John looked much better than he had three days before. His bruises, while far more colorful, weren't nearly as angry looking. He no longer winced at sudden movements, and whatever had caused the limp had only been visible when he'd tucked his long frame into the car.

"Why did you choose this car anyway?" she asked, needing, wanting, to find an outlet for her frustration and fear. "If I'm uncomfortable, you must be cramping up big time. And a shiny little road machine isn't something that blends in."

"Exactly." He didn't look at her.

She pressed on. "Ah. Ever the strategist. Hide in plain sight."

"Actually, T. J. was responsible for the car."

"Such a kidder, T. J."

John slowly turned his head, pinning her with

frustratingly unreadable eyes. Suddenly returning to their silent truce was intolerable.

"Why did we agree to this, McShane? I know you aren't any happier to be on baby-sitting detail than I am being baby-sat."

He slowly eased a breath out and leaned back in the seat. He shifted his gaze back to the windshield.

When he didn't speak, she said, "I know, I know. We didn't have any choice." He let his eyes slide shut. She tensed, not wanting him to retreat from her. She was loath to admit it at the moment, even to herself, but though she didn't need him as her watchdog, she did need him. As a man. As a partner. As a friend. As the only one to whom she felt she could turn. He'd always been that man.

The full impact of that revelation was too hot to handle at the moment. She rushed on, knowing she was babbling and not caring as long as it filled the silence, pushed back the building tension between them. "Scottie can be a real bulldog. I can see why she was chosen to take over. But with your team so under-manned, it makes no sense to send us out to traipse around the countryside when we could be helping."

"Both of us would be more hindrance than help to her. Her intuition was sharper than I'd credited her for."

He'd spoken in a low, even voice that startled her into momentary silence. There was no question he'd meant every word he'd said.

"If you agree with her decision, then why are you acting like someone spit in your cornflakes?"

"Because she was right."

Cali opened her mouth, then shut it again. She tried to sort it out but quickly gave up. Her brain felt like scrambled eggs from staring at too many strings of numbers and symbols, and her emotions would look about the same if they could be drafted into code.

She forced herself to relax back into the leather bucket seat, purposely easing some of the tension she'd summoned up to replace the strength and control she no longer had. "You really think you would have hurt the mission?"

He opened his eyes and shifted his head to look at her. There was an emotion in his eyes, but she had no clue what it was.

"I know I would have," he stated flatly. He lifted his hand from the wheel when she would have spoken. He placed it loosely on the gearshift, focusing on the white pattern etched in the surface of the knob as if it held the answers to some ancient secret. His shift of focus, that he spoke without looking at her, told her a lot about his state of mind. Rarely if ever did John McShane not meet a task head-on, no matter how difficult.

"Why?" she asked, pushing, knowing this time she wouldn't stop. It would all come out now. "Because of me?" Her voice lowered, softened. "Because I'd have jeopardized your role in this with my inexperience?"

"Yes, because of you." He traced the gearshift pattern again, then finally dragged his gaze to hers. "But not because of your inability to help. What you've done in this whole thing has been nothing short of amazing. You've earned the respect of all of us, and that's not something to take lightly."

His praise filled her with warmth, but she stayed focused on the other, unexplained part. "Then why—"

"Because of my inability to put the job first." He shifted, sitting up and looking straight at her. "Because my judgment was governed by my feelings for you and not what was best for the team or for getting the job done. Scottie knew that if push came to shove, I'd sacrifice the damn program and everything else just to keep you safe."

"But wh—"

He let go of the shift knob and took her hand, turning her palm against his. She watched him slowly weave his fingers through hers. When the warmth of his palm and wrist touched hers, she instinctively, instantly, tightened her grip until she felt their pulses mingle and race on.

This time it was she who slowly dragged her gaze up to his, both frightened and excited at what she might find in those gray depths.

Her fingers convulsively clutched and loosened at the stark emotion she found there, bared to the soul for her to see. She would have pulled away, the instinct to somehow fortify her barriers stronger than the need to meld her strength with his, but he was faster, held her fingers firmly within his grasp.

He looked down at their entwined fingers, then

pulled them up to his mouth and kissed her knuckles. His eyes closed and he rested his mouth against the back of her hand. She felt more than heard him swear softly.

She cupped his head with her other hand, ruffled her fingers into his hair. And waited. She'd pushed, she'd prodded, she'd bullied. Maybe it was time to back off and let him find his own way.

A few seconds went by. It seemed like hours. Then he lifted his head and tugged on her hand, simultaneously reaching behind him with his other one and opening his door.

"I need to get out of here. Walk with me?"

In that moment she'd have laid down her life for him. He already had for her. "Yes."

He let go of her hand for as long as it took them to climb out of the car. He met her at the trunk and, to her great relief, took her hand again as he led her down the dirt track, farther away from the main road.

After several silent moments she asked, "Do you know where we are?"

"Other than what state we're in and what highway we're on, I haven't a clue."

He sounded somewhat pleased about that. Cali felt her mouth curve into a smile and let the feeling in. She forced herself not to fill in the silence, instead focusing on the sounds of the birds and the breeze rustling through the trees and tall grasses. It was still early fall and the air was quite warm but fresh. There were few clouds in the sky. Her smile grew pensive as her thoughts and senses zeroed in on the man walking beside her.

No, she thought, there were plenty of clouds. They were all inside John McShane. She slowly shifted closer to him as they continued to walk.

Their pace was slow but steady. The countryside rolled out over a wide grassy field that didn't seem to end until it hit the mountains in the distance. She glanced over at John. His profile wasn't as harsh, but he was far from relaxed. The tension and strain were still evident in the pinched skin around his eyes and tightness at the corners of his mouth. And there was no escaping the bruises and scrapes that marred his beautiful face.

"Why do you do it?" She hadn't meant to speak, had truly meant to let him set the pace. But she couldn't help it. She had no idea what John wanted from her, needed from her, but pretending to be something she wasn't wouldn't help either of them. "What makes you go out there and put your life on the line?"

He let the question hang in the warm breeze for so long, she thought he wouldn't answer her. Then he said quite simply, "Because I can. Because I'm good at it." He didn't look at her, but his fingers tightened a bit. "Because, as unfortunate as it is, there's a need for people like me to do this." He paused, then added, "And it's the only way I've found I can let myself be needed."

"People like you?"

"Loners. People who can remain insular. Not many can."

The revelation didn't surprise her; that he'd shared it with her had. It occurred to her that she knew very little about him. "Isn't there anyone you need, anyone who needs you? What about family?"

"I have none. None left, anyway. I was a late-life surprise to my parents. My dad was in the military, so we never stayed in one place too long."

"No ties," she murmured.

He nodded. "My mom was the quintessential military wife. Everything she did was for my father and his career. I'm not sure she ever knew quite what to do with me. I don't think she could figure out how being a mother could fit in with the role she'd assigned herself in his life. He was proud to have a son, though, so she took that and ran with it. It was our job to make him proud of us."

"They sound pretty self-involved." He glanced at her. "I don't necessarily mean that as a indictment," she said. "I didn't know them. Just . . . Were you ever close to either of them?"

"I loved them." He looked ahead, down the path. "But no, I wasn't. Not in the way I think you mean. They've both been gone for a long time. Since before I joined the Circle. I was in the army when they died."

"Was that to make your dad proud too?"

She was surprised but pleased to see his lips curve a bit. "In a way. Dad was air force."

Cali smiled dryly. "I'm shocked."

He glanced at her. "Yeah, right. I guess you better than anyone can relate to parental pressure and expectations." He grinned. "Not that you would ever do anything rebellious."

His smile made her skin heat, her heart pound, and her thighs tighten up a bit. The man could turn on the charm.

"Not me," she responded, struggling to keep her tone dry and teasing. They walked on in silence, each of their gazes drifting to the dirt track. Her thoughts slowly spun inward. She thought of what his life had been like. "I guess it's tough to form attachments, build relationships, without the foundation for it."

He squeezed her hand. A hot thrill raced up her arm. She liked connecting with him, liked that he felt it too.

"Probably not as hard as I made it," he said. "Lot's of people have older parents; even more are military brats. I got used to taking care of myself, relying on myself. I made friends okay, I just never stayed in one place long enough to keep them. And that held true in the military as well. I still connect with people around me; I operate better that way."

"Like Nathan."

He nodded. "And others. You close yourself completely off and you get out of touch with what makes people tick. In my line of work, you need to have that sensitivity." He shrugged. "I don't let myself rely on them, that's all."

"That's no small thing."

"No. But it's easier. I think one of the reasons I

joined the Circle was because it emphasized those very qualities. It sort of gave me permission to stay that way, not to take those risks."

Cali laughed.

He glanced sharply at her. "What's so funny about that?"

"I think it's interesting that you feel safer in an environment where you risk your life rather than your heart."

He tugged her to a stop, turning her to face him. His expression was so serious, she sobered instantly. "I was merely making an observation," she said gently. "Not passing judgment. I'd be the last person to do that."

"You're right. It is easier to risk my life. Much more controlled and calculated."

"Have you ever risked your heart?"

She felt his hold on her hands gradually increase in pressure, but wasn't sure he realized it.

"Only once. I'd rather risk my life. I understand that territory."

Now it was she who had to take a risk. She understood now what he meant. Terrified, with no road map to guide her, no guarantee of what she would find upon arriving, she found herself too intrigued, too tempted, to turn back. Her only option was to take the plunge.

"What happened?"

He reached up and stroked her cheek. His touch was achingly gentle. "The heart mine wanted was already taken."

She felt her eyes burn at the dull pain she heard underlying his words. Pain he'd lived with for a long time, judging by the sounds of it. "I'm sorry." She meant it. She'd only had Nathan for a short time, but it had been worth it despite its painfully abrupt end. She stopped herself short of wondering who John had wanted so badly. It was far too easy to project herself into that role.

Still, she heard herself say, "There are many other hearts out there, John." Her own ached.

"Tell that to mine." He slid his fingertips over her lips, pressing them shut when she would have spoken. "It's only ever wanted one."

Her voice caught in her throat, along with her breath. He didn't mean, couldn't . . . But he was talking about his past. And their past had been during the time she'd been married to— Her eyes widened. *The heart I wanted was already taken.*

No. She was mistaken. She was reading too much into his expression. It was fatigue and stress making her fanciful. It was need and want, she told herself. She swallowed, still unable to speak. Ridiculous. He couldn't have felt that way. . . .

But it explained too many things. In fact, it explained everything.

He dropped her hand and turned away. She reached out, snagged his hand, and tugged him back.

"What do you mean?" she demanded. "And no more talking in circles."

He swore under his breath, then looked back to her. "See, this is why I don't do this."

"Do what?"

"Put my heart out there. It scares the daylights out of me."

Even as her heart began to pound, as her mind clamored to believe he was talking about her, joy began to bubble inside her. Joy and hope. How long had it been since she'd taken this sweet, scary thrill ride? Ten years, she acknowledged.

Well, her inner voice queried, *isn't it about time to buy another ticket?*

Scared to death and loving it, a small, knowing, entirely female smile curved her lips. "Join the crowd, McShane."

He frowned. "What do you mean?"

"Do you think it's ever easy? That no one else ever feels like this, the loss of control, the scary 'I'm stepping off a cliff and what if no one catches me?' feeling?"

"Feels like this?" he repeated. "What do you think I feel?" His grip on her shoulders tightened. "What do you feel?"

Her heart was pounding so hard now, she could barely hear her own jumbled thoughts, much less his low purr of a voice. "Not fair, McShane." Her voice wavered. She tried to step back, but he pulled her closer.

His knees brushed her thighs, his hips pressed above hers. She felt him, hard and warm and strong. She wanted to lean into him, melt into him. She trembled and tried desperately to put together a decent sentence and lock her knees to keep them from buckling at the same time.

"You started this discussion," she said as he moved even closer. "You first."

"Look at me, Cali."

Oh God, she thought. Ten years. Here I am at the edge of the cliff again. She was afraid to look, afraid to see how high up she was this time.

His grip gentled, his fingers stroked her shoulders to the base of her neck. "Maybe it's easier if we both go at the same time." His voice gentled with his touch. "I'll catch you if you catch me."

He prodded her with his fingers. She looked up. "Deal."

He lowered his mouth to hers. His lips were warm, his tongue, as it slid into her mouth, was hot and wet. She slid her arm around his waist. He flinched and she immediately tried to move away.

"No, don't," he said against her mouth. He pulled her hand back around his waist. "I'm just a little sore, that's all."

She smoothed her palm across his lower back and eased herself closer to him.

A deep sigh rose inside him and escaped slowly. Cali felt herself sigh too.

"That's it, Cali." He let her hand go and slid his arms around her, pulling her tightly into his embrace. He nuzzled aside the hair by her ear and kissed her neck. "Don't ever let me go." His words were a dark whisper, filled with need.

Cali heard that, felt it inside her soul. She lifted

her lips to his chin, then his jaw, then his neck. She worked her way to his ear, thrilling at the trembling shimmer she felt race over him as she bit softly on his earlobe. "I need you, too, John McShane. I need you too."

He groaned and took her mouth hard and fast. Her legs were shaking, and she clutched at him as she returned his kiss. She felt at once wild and reckless and connected and cared for.

As his mouth moved to the soft skin above her collarbone, his hands slid up her waist and around front and cupped her breasts. The moan rose and erupted from deep within her as his fingers flicked softly over her tightened nipples. Her knees buckled, and he caught her to him, turning both of them around as they stumble-walked into the thick, green grass. She couldn't have said who pulled whom down, but they were sprawled in the grass and on each other before her thoughts formed any sort of rational pattern.

John slid her T-shirt from her jeans and pushed it up and over her bra. He flicked the front open before she could grab it and wrench it off.

"God, I've never needed like this." She was panting.

He suckled first one nipple, then the other, eliciting moans from someplace deep inside her.

"Join the club, Ellis," he said, echoing her earlier words, his voice all rumbly and deep against the ultrasensitive skin he was stroking with his lips.

She moved enough to get her shirt off. He pulled

his off, flipped it behind him, rolled to his back, and pulled her on top of him. The sight of the black-and-blue marks marring his muscled chest and ribs made her gasp and had her trying to lever her weight off of him. He instantly clamped her tightly to him.

"But your ribs, and—"

"I meant what I said. I've waited ten years for you to turn to me. Don't let me go now, Cali."

She trembled at the bare intensity of his words, his stark need. She brushed her fingertips over one particularly nasty welt. "But you're hurt." She looked at him, eyes burning. "Because of me. I can't—"

"I'm only feeling pain in one place right now," he said, then shut up any further protests with another soul-shattering kiss.

Cali understood that pain. As he slid his tongue across her throat and back down to her nipples, she slid her hand between them, grappling for the button at the waistband of her jeans. She encountered John's hand fumbling for his. Between them they managed to get zippers down and jeans pushed over hips.

The friction of his skin against hers, heightened by their joint struggles, only pushed her desire higher. The heat threatened to consume her and she thought she'd explode if she didn't do something to assuage the pain from the tight clenching of the muscles between her legs. She smoothed her palm over his hips and cupped him, then wrapped her hand around him. He arched. She groaned.

"I need you, John. Now."

Through clenched teeth he said, "Another second

of your hand wrapped around me, and now will be then real quick."

"Then let's make it now, right now." She released him and moved her body over his, straddling the hard length she'd caressed moments ago.

With a large palm on the back of her neck, he pulled her mouth down to his and took her with his tongue in the same driving rhythm she was using as she slid her wet heat back and forth over him. The ache wound tighter until it became hot, physical pain. She was panting now, then gasping as he shifted her up so he could lever his mouth over her nipple once again.

"I'm gonna die."

"Yeah," he growled against the moist skin between her breasts.

What remaining breath she had evaporated. "That'll teach me to make love with a man who's not afraid of dying," she said on a rapidly whispered exhale.

"I am now," he said. His unexpected gentle kiss melted what was left of her heart. "Guess that's what happens when you have something to live for."

"Oh, John."

"Take me, Cali."

And she did. He moved inside her, full and hot and hard, filling her excruciatingly and wonderfully slowly, allowing her to savor and shudder through each second of deliciously wicked sensation. He built it up from there.

She moved against him, their increasing rhythm as

natural as if they'd bonded the same way a thousand times before. Her hands gripped his shoulders, then slid to cup his face as she lowered her face to just above his. His eyes were fierce and burning with some inner light, a depth of emotion she'd never thought to witness in him. She suspected if she'd had a mirror at that moment, she'd find the same emotions in hers. Never before, not even with Nathan, had she felt so strong a bond. Not once did they need to speak, not once did they break eye contact.

And it was there that she found a connection more powerful than the physical joining of their bodies. other. It was there she found the other half of herself. It was there, in those smoky gray depths, that she found her soul.

As if to prove the truth of that power, the instant that realization hit her, he surged more deeply inside her. She tilted her head back only to feel his hands on her face, pulling her back to him. "You have my heart, Cali. Only you. Always you." His growl started low inside him and built as he pushed harder, deeper. With a groan he came inside her.

Dazed as much by his words as by the pleasure still assaulting her body, she needed a moment to realize he hadn't stopped moving. "John?"

His mouth curved ever so slightly, but this time the teasing half smile reached his eyes. Oh, she could love this man. She wanted his heart. Always.

It scared her to death.

He kept moving. So did she.

"Your turn," he murmured.

"It's—"

"Shhh." He loosened his hold enough to roll her gently to her back, pull her underneath him, and move deeply into her.

"Open your eyes."

She did. The rush she got from seeing the naked emotion on his face, the raw honesty, almost sent her over the edge.

"Come to me, Cali."

He pulled her thighs up, shifted her hips, drove into her one more time. And she did as he asked.

ELEVEN

John rolled to his side, pulled Cali's thigh up over his, and cradled her in his arms. The urge to protect her was as fierce as the urge to take her, claim her, had been. He knew she had been moved as deeply as he had been, but that didn't help to bank the panic slowly building inside him.

He held on tighter.

Instead of squirming, she snuggled closer.

Despite their position, he realized he felt protected too. His throat closed over. She'd claimed him just as surely as he had her. Instead of being reassured, he was terrified.

"There *is* magic here." Her words were a warm breath against his chest.

"Hmm?" was as coherent a sound as he could make.

She looked up at him, smiling, eyes shining. Oh, how he loved this woman. How he'd always loved her.

And now that he'd given in to it, taken her with him . . . how in the hell would he ever walk away?

Worse, how in the hell could he stay?

"Magic circles," she explained.

He mentally grabbed onto her words, focused with everything he had, hoping to keep the desperation crawling inside him at bay.

"It's the way I felt as a child when I was with my dad. Like as long as he was nearby, nothing bad would happen to me." She traced lazy patterns on his skin as she talked. "Then later, with Nathan, I felt as if nothing could intrude or spoil what we had. The baby only solidified that feeling." Her fingers stilled, but her gaze didn't waver. "After they died, I stopped believing in magic circles."

Hopelessness and panic clawed at this throat, at his heart. Not because he was afraid to step into her magic circle, but because he wanted it as he'd never allowed himself to want anything in his life. And he didn't see how he could take it.

"That's not such a bad way to think," he said. "You're just being wise."

She levered up on one elbow. "That's what I thought. I thought I'd finally grown up, finally understood life from a mature, adult perspective instead of with childish innocence."

"Understandably so. What happened to you would make an adult out of just about anyone."

"That's just it. It wasn't about being adult. It was about being cynical. You know what I realized? Most people believe that life is one long endless road littered with potholes, some small, some huge enough to swallow you whole. These same people feel lucky if they happen to avoid one now and then, but they are certain they're going to fall into a good number of them. Such a pessimistic view of the world, don't you think? And I was one of those people.

"The weird thing is, I realize there is some safety in believing the 'life usually sucks' theory. Then you don't have to be responsible for your own happiness. If things go wrong, well, 'that's life.' "

"But there is truth to that, Cali. You don't have control over most things."

She leaned over his chest, her green eyes almost electric with emotion. "That doesn't mean you give up on everything else."

She sat up. His gaze ran over her naked torso, covered only in the bright sunlight.

"What we're feeling right now has nothing to do with playing it safe. You know what this feeling is?"

"Abject terror?"

She smiled, then laughed. "Yes, it is. And wild and exhilarating and anything but safe. What we're feeling is alive, John McShane." She pushed him on his back and gently straddled his waist, taking his hands and pinning them over his head. He let her. Hell, right then he'd have let her do anything she wanted. Because she was right, he did feel alive, in a way he'd never known he could.

It scared the daylights out of him.

For the first time he realized that it may not be such a bad thing.

"I thought I was being smart. In the last ten years I've been physically healthy. I've been financially successful. But emotionally? I've had nothing. I don't want to go back into my pessimistic cocoon. I want to believe in magic circles again, John. I want to risk hitting a pothole. Because then I'll know I'm going down the road instead of being forever stalled at some safe little rest stop along the way."

John smiled up at her. It was impossible not to. "How did we get into this road stuff anyway?"

She grinned. "Considering where we are literally, it seemed a good analogy."

He pushed at her hands, broke free, and pulled her down on top of him, nestling her face against his neck.

Alive. "I do feel it, Cali."

"Mmmm." She kissed his neck and snuggled closer. "Wrap your arms around me."

He did, even as he said, "I'm just not sure if I can be your magic circle." She immediately tried to sit up, but he wouldn't let her. He held her close, burying his nose in her hair, closing his eyes and inhaling her scent, hoping to find some way to express himself so she'd understand. "I want to be. In fact I don't think I've ever wanted or needed to be anything for anyone as badly as I want to be everything for you. Everything you need me to be."

She pulled in a deep breath, then let it out slowly. "But?" she said against the crook of his neck.

"How can I? Our past . . ." He blew out a frustrated sigh. "I wanted you when you belonged to my best friend, my partner. Hell, I wanted you when you had just lost his child."

She snaked her arms around him and held him tightly. "Nathan's gone, John."

"Lord, Cali, don't you get it? It's not that simple. I'm not your magic circle. I'm everything that you are fighting against. I'm cynical, I'm pessimistic. I've seen too much of the bad side of life. I've been the bad side of yours. I'm one of those people who believes in potholes."

She pulled her head free of his grasp and looked at him, her eyes were glassy. "But that's just it, John. This isn't about the past. If it was, then I could never get out of the hole I buried myself in after Nathan and the baby died. You weren't the cause of that. In fact, you were the one who helped me. If I didn't still feel that way, I wouldn't have come to you for help this time." She braced her palms on either side of his head. "You get to choose. You can let life happen to you, or you can take the risk." She locked her gaze to his. "I think you're worth it. I want you in my life, John McShane."

"I don't have a life to give you, Cali." He shook his head when she started to argue. "No. I don't. I left the only life I've ever known. I have no idea what I'm going to do. I'm physically worn down. I'm fiscally unsure. And emotionally . . . Hell, I'm in such new territory there, I need a map to find my way out."

"Would finding your way out with me make you happy?"

He blew out a frustrated breath and rolled her off

of him. He sat up and braced his elbows on his bent knees. "Dammit, Cali, don't you understand? You need someone who can grab onto this new life you want and run with it. How can I do that when I don't know where I'm going? It's not about what will make me happy."

"It's a good place to start."

He swore under his breath and grabbed for his jeans. Without saying anything, Cali dressed. When she rolled to a stand, he reached for her before she could walk away.

"I'm sorry."

She looked up into his eyes. He thought he might see pity. What he saw was sorrow and pain. "I'm not trying to hurt you."

Her eyes flared. "Well, I think you're doing a damn fine job of hurting both of us."

"I'm sorry for that too. I'm trying to be honest. It's the only thing I have to hang on to right now."

She reached up and stroked his face. "Then I do feel sorry for you, John. You still don't see what is right in front of your face. You say you've wanted me for ten years. You have a hell of a funny way of showing it."

She turned and walked away from him.

"Maybe it's because I love you so much that I can't risk disappointing you."

She stopped dead, then slowly turned around. "If you love me, then how can you not try? What exactly are you afraid of, McShane?"

Because he had no answer, he was forced to watch her turn and walk away.

Cali slumped down in the car seat and waited for John to return. When several minutes passed and there was still no sign of him, she gave serious consideration to leaving him behind. But a quick glance showed he'd taken the car keys. She did not want to think about what had happened between them. Nor did she want to think about the rest of what was going on in her life at the moment. Which left her future. She'd purposely shoved that to the side since she'd left for Martinique. She had nothing to return to except an empty apartment. Granted, she had insurance money, both her own to cover the theft and what was left of Nathan's after all her travel expenses.

But she couldn't seem to drum up any enthusiasm for shopping or rebuilding the rest of her life. She'd left clients in the lurch when she'd gone on the run. She'd been afraid to contact anyone for fear of leaving any trail, or worse, putting innocent people in the path of the men who were after her.

So not only was her personal life a complete shambles, her professional life didn't look too promising either.

Sighing, she reached for her backpack, intent on finding the packet of mints she'd tucked in the side. What she found instead was a somewhat worse-for-wear photograph. She hadn't put it in there. But she knew as she turned it over to look at the front who had.

It was the snapshot she'd sent to John. The one taken of her and Nathan in front of the bungalow. She stared at the photo, smiled sadly as she remembered that day. She had been happy, had felt as if her whole life was in front of her. She'd felt . . . free.

She'd thought Nathan had given her that. The freedom to truly break free and do what she wanted. But she knew now she had given it to herself. Since his death, she'd never really freed herself again. She rubbed a fingertip over his smile as she thought about all the life plans they'd made in that bungalow.

The driver's-side door opened and she shoved the photo away.

All John said was, "Get your seat belt on." They were swerving onto the highway before she had the clasp hooked.

She held on to the door handle and the dashboard with equal fervor. "Where are we going, John? I think I have a right to know."

"There's been a change of plans."

"Considering I didn't know the original plan—"

"I got a cell call."

Which explained why he'd taken so long coming back to the car. And she thought he'd been agonizing over her. More fool she.

She'd been there when Scottie had given him the high-tech phone. Apparently it was a creation of their former leader, specialized in that it scrambled the transmission so no one could listen in on a conversation. Spy toys.

"Did they catch them? Is it over?" She tried to keep the hope from her voice.

"No."

She sighed in frustration but swallowed her retort when she noticed his white-knuckled grip on the steering wheel.

Quietly she asked, "What happened, John?"

He paused, but only for a second. "T. J. He's hurt. There's no one to go in after him."

Realization came swiftly. "Except you."

He nodded sharply.

"But Scottie said—"

"The hell with what Scottie said. You don't know what he got me out of, Cali. I can't just let him—" He broke off and shoved his foot down on the gas pedal.

Cali swallowed hard, the still-brutal-looking bruises marking his beautiful body agonizingly clear in her mind's eye. "So where do we go to get him?"

"That's the change in plans. I don't have much time."

An ominous feeling settled heavily in her chest. "So where are we going?"

"Airstrip, just ahead."

Her eyes narrowed further. "We're taking a trip?"

"Not exactly." He hadn't looked at her once.

Cali didn't have to drag the whole thing out of him, she saw the scenario pretty clearly. "So you were going to ship me off somewhere so you could run back and join your buddies all along."

His silence was answer enough. Eyes glued to the road, he took another tight curve with gravity-bending speed.

Cali hesitated before hashing it out any further for fear she'd distract him, and after all of this, they'd both end up roadkill in the middle of nowhere. But patience had never been her strong suit.

"Answer me, McShane. Does Scottie know about this? Was this the real plan all along?" She'd been in on all the final instructions, and to her knowledge, John was to stay with her until it was all over—the only aspect of the plan she'd approved of. Of course, she realized now, there could have been other meetings she knew nothing about.

He glanced at her.

"You bastard."

He turned his attention back to the highway. "I've told you that before about me."

She didn't know which emotion won out—fury or hurt. It didn't matter, her control snapped. "Where are you sending me? I thought you all couldn't trust anyone? The only other person who knows anything—" Her eyes widened. "No. No, you wouldn't." She didn't care if she killed them both, she reached out and dug her nails into his arm. "Tell me you're not sending me to my father."

He didn't flinch under her assault. "There was no other way. The embassy can afford us protection that we couldn't ensure anywhere else."

One word snagged her attention. "*Us?* Do you

expect me to believe you really intend to get on the plane?"

"It was my intention."

"Until now."

He slowed down marginally and looked at her. "I have to go back for T. J., Cali."

"Then take me with you."

"I can't do that."

"Then stop the car."

"Don't, Cali. This whole thing will be over soon. You won't have to stay at the embassy more than a couple of weeks."

"Just when were you going to tell me?"

"At about twenty-thousand feet. Where I knew you couldn't pull a stunt like you want to pull now."

She hated the fact that his plan had been right on, because she would have tried to bail out. "What makes you think you can get me on that plane now?"

He slowed the car completely and pulled over. "Because there is no way I'm going to let you anywhere near the action. You've been as close to a fired bullet as you're going to get. Let the team take down Adrian Magdelane. He, or someone he works for—Grimshaw, most likely—tried to kill you. He probably had something to do with Nathan's accident too. Whatever you feel for me or think of me, don't put me through this, Cali."

"If you're so damned worried about me, then why were you so eager to get rid of me?"

"Nothing else has changed, Cali. I didn't lie about how I feel. I also didn't lie about what I think is best."

"Yeah, but best for me or for you?"

He stared at her for a long time, then very quietly said, "I wish I knew."

It wasn't his words, but the true anguish she saw in his eyes that extinguished her anger and will to fight. "I don't suppose there is anywhere else on the face of the earth you can hide me until this is over?"

To his credit, he didn't show any relief at her unspoken decision.

"If there was, I'd have found it. I want you safe."

"Make me one promise."

"If I can."

"When this is all over, I get a full report on exactly what happened. Especially since it involved Nathan."

A flash of pain crossed John's features and his hand reflexively gripped the gear knob. Despite her lingering anger, Cali felt her eyes burn. She smoothed her fingers over the now rigid veins in his arms. "He'd be proud of you, John. Of all that you've done. For both of us."

He didn't say anything, didn't move so much as a hair.

Cali swore silently, knowing it was time to shut up but unable to. "He'd also want me to be happy. You too. Don't let a ghost stand in the way, McShane. When this is over, put it all to rest."

In answer, he shifted her hand from his arm and pulled back on the road. Hurt mixed with pain, but she bit her lip and remained silent. Several minutes passed, then several more.

"I want to know about T. J. too," she said quietly. "I understand why you have to go back for him."

He slowed for a second and looked directly at her. "I would have gotten on the plane, Cali."

She simply nodded. There was nothing else left to say.

TWELVE

John paced the twentieth-floor Denver office that had once belonged to Seve Delgado but was now temporary home to Scottie Giardi. She was late.

He stared out the floor-to-ceiling window behind the massive desk, too preoccupied to see the majesty of the Rockies laid out before him. He hadn't been informed about why he was there, although he could make a pretty good guess.

"Well, Ms. Giardi is going to have to learn to take no for an answer," he muttered. He turned away from the window and paced the considerable length of the office. Scottie had taken the idea of rebuilding the team to heart. She was not only scouting for new team members, but also changing the way the team operated. She wanted a permanent interior staff of trained operatives as well as field agents. Her rationale was to prevent what had happened when Del left from happening again. This would give the team depth and a broader base of power.

John approved. Had told her so. He just didn't want to be a part of it. Problem was, he had no idea what he did want to be a part of. It had been two months since they'd brought in the fringe team that formed inside the Blue Circle, calling themselves the Inner Circle. They had restructured themselves as an internal band of Uncle Sam's finest who had their own code for success. They had been operating for their own gain for well over ten years. Having Nathan's program become available again had been too tempting to pass up. The possibility of retiring the entire team in luxury and wealth as a result of selling the program to the highest international bidder had caused them to get sloppy, impatient, and they'd gone after Cali.

In the end, she had been the one to bring about their downfall. She'd been right on about Adrian being the connection. Once the team had brought him in, it had been only matter of time before the rest were rounded up. Trial dates still hung in the far future, but for now, Cali was safe. And the virus program had been rendered inactive with an antidote program.

He hadn't seen Cali since he'd sent her off in that plane. She'd stayed away for several weeks, then returned to L.A. He knew that she'd made a stop in Denver to be debriefed. She'd been told, along with all the other gritty details, that he had successfully extricated T. J., though his teammate had sustained injuries serious enough to require some lengthy hospitalization. John had talked with Scottie and T. J.

The only one he hadn't heard from was Cali. Not once.

Not that he'd expected to. He swore under his breath and paced back to the window. Her words still rang in his ears. *What exactly are you afraid of, John McShane?*

The door opened behind him. He swung around just as Scottie crossed the threshold.

"If you dragged me here to talk me into being internal strategic coordinator, you could have saved the airfare—"

He broke off when another person entered the room.

Cali.

In that moment he realized he knew the answer. Had known it all along. He'd been afraid he wouldn't survive if he allowed himself to want her, had her, then lost her again. But hadn't that already happened?

Scottie walked briskly to her desk, leaving Cali pausing in the doorway. Apparently she knew nothing about this little meeting either.

"Sorry to keep you waiting." Scottie sat in the large burgundy leather chair and rolled up to the desk. "Cali and I had some last-minute details to hammer out." She looked from one to the other then glanced down at her blotter. John thought she might have grinned, but he found his attention pulled back to the doorway.

Scottie pinned both of them with a no-nonsense

look and gestured to the two navy leather chairs across from her. "Well, have a seat. I'm due at another meeting in less than ten minutes."

Cali stepped in, her long russet skirt brushing her ankles when she sat. She crossed her arms over a thick, cream-colored cowl sweater and turned her attention to Scottie. John found himself following suit, though he had a harder time forcing his attention to his former boss.

Scottie snapped open a folder and pulled out two thick sheaves of papers. She slid the slightly thinner one across the desk toward Cali and the other toward John. "Here is the final outline of the proposed restructuring of the new Dirty Dozen." She looked to Cali as they both picked up their copies. "You know most of this. Familiarize yourself with the rest. Any questions John can't answer, save for the first meeting." She shifted to John, not giving him time to assimilate her words much less comment on them. "My proposal for your position is all there. It's my final offer. I think I have covered everything that might be of a concern to you. I want you as part of this team, John, and I'm not above using any means to get you. You might be interested to know that Santerra has agreed to meet with me to discuss his becoming our in-house special-skills trainer. That's where I'm headed now, in fact." She nodded at the papers he held. "I think you'll see that I mean business." She flipped her folder closed, scooted her chair back, and stood. "Please don't add to my workload and make me replace you."

She rounded the desk and stuck out her hand to Cali, who also rose and shook it. "Welcome to the team, Agent Ellis." She jerked her head toward John. "I'd say I was sorry for the surprise, but I'm not." She flashed a sudden, brilliant smile that was stunning in its transformation of her demeanor. "Now's your shot, Cali. Don't you blow it, either."

She strode to the door, had one hand on the knob when John finally found his feet and his voice. He had questions. A lot of them. He fully intended to get answers to each one of them, but first things first. "Scottie."

She turned, raising a questioning brow.

He'd lost too much in the past by not saying what was in his heart when he should have. This was as good a place to turn over a new leaf as any. "Regardless of my decision, Del would be proud of you. We all are."

A faint trace of color on her cheeks was her only reaction. She was a leader already.

"It takes all of us, John. Don't let him down."

"Low blow, Agent Giardi. You still backing out after you reorganize?"

"Touché, Agent McShane." She smiled; this time it seemed less spontaneous and more than a bit intimidating. "But for the record, when you report to work next week, you can call me boss." She was gone before he could so much as nod his approval.

"Does that mean you're on the team again?" Cali asked.

He turned to face her. "It means I think she'll make a helluva boss."

He let himself truly look at her. In less than five minutes the entire foundation of his world had shifted, and as was becoming the rule rather than the exception, Cali Ellis was in the center of it.

This time he felt as if he'd been handed the proverbial second chance—at his whole life. And he had no idea what to do to make sure he didn't blow it. Again.

"I take it you're part of the new Dozen?" He wasn't sure how he felt about that.

She nodded. "And don't worry, despite what Scottie hinted at, I wasn't brought in as bait to get you back. I made sure of that myself. I wouldn't have wanted her to waste her time."

"Don't let her fool you. She'd resort to whatever methods were at her disposal to get what she wanted."

"Why haven't you taken the job? I would have thought this would have been the perfect solution."

It should have been. He certainly didn't have other offers pouring in. But he couldn't commit to it. For the past several months he'd felt . . . empty. In fact, he could pinpoint the exact moment when the feeling had begun—the second the door to the small charter plane had closed, the final barrier between him and Cali.

"Is that why you took the job?"

She lifted an eyebrow but merely smiled as she crossed her arms. "I see your super-secret-spy ego is still intact. And for the record, I don't think my job rides on my ability to reel you in. I hold my own here."

"What is your position with the team?"

Her smile held steady. "Sorry, McShane, but that's classified information, known only to other team members."

He hadn't expected this to be easy. Frustrated but determined not to let it get the best of him, he crossed to the window, turning his attention to the magnificent skyline. "Well then, I guess you'd better go. Looks like you have some heavy reading to do."

"No answer, then?"

"I don't know what I want to do, Cali. At the risk of showing that ego you spoke of, I imagine if I want to work with the team at some point in the future, Scottie will find a place for me."

"And in the meantime?"

He had no answer. She had been his meantime. She'd occupied most of his waking thoughts and all of his sleeping ones. And now there she was, several feet away from him. There to touch, caress, stroke. A couple of steps away from holding, tasting, needing. In all the time they'd been apart he'd never figured out what he'd say to her if he saw her again. Divine inspiration wasn't coming to his assistance now either. He'd told her he loved her. She'd thrown it back in his face. He'd told her he had no plans for his future. Not a good selling point.

So what in the hell could he say to make her understand he wanted her?

Maybe it didn't matter how difficult she made it

for him. Maybe there were no second chances. Maybe he didn't deserve one.

"I'm glad you found something that could make you happy, Cali."

There was a long silence. He tried to see her reflection in the glass, but the angle of the setting sun was wrong. He wanted to turn, but didn't trust himself to move one inch for fear he'd cross the room and take her in his arms and kiss her senseless.

"I'm looking forward to the challenge," she said after a long pause. There was no smug amusement in her voice now. "But I don't know about happy."

He did turn. "What's to be unhappy about? You don't like Denver?"

She shook her head. "Denver is okay. I'm surprised, but I like all this snow. Guess I've been in California long enough."

"Your father still giving you trouble?"

She sighed softly but shook her head again. "Some of the decisions I made during our time together seemed to have stuck. I handled my father better than I thought I could." A hint of the smile returned. "Better than he thought too."

He was certain he was opening himself up to pain, but what the hell did he have to lose? "Well then, what is it?" He allowed himself a small step toward her.

To his relief, she stood her ground.

"What else do you want, Cali?"

"I'm not sure. I guess I'm getting it now."

"Meaning?"

"I thought I'd be okay if I could see you one more time, talk to you. I thought that would somehow make it easier. I'm not sure I was right."

The bare hint of hurt in her voice had him taking another step, curling his fingers into his palms to keep from reaching for her. "Right about what? Make what easier?"

She didn't answer. After a long moment she looked away, lacing her fingers. It was the first less-than-certain reaction he'd seen in her.

"In case you were wondering, I'm not pregnant."

He'd thought about that. He'd hoped like hell she'd have contacted him if she was. Still, hearing it from her shook him. He wasn't sure what to do with the overwhelming sensation of disappointment that flooded through him.

She looked up before he had a chance to mask his expression.

"Thank you for telling me," he said quietly. "I worried about you."

"Yeah, all those cards and phone calls were a real nuisance."

Her sharp tone caught him by surprise. He answered without taking time to think it through. "Scottie said you'd already been debriefed by the time I came in. After that I didn't hear from you either. What the hell was I supposed to do, Cali? Call up and say, 'Hi, how was the Middle East? Oh, by the way, you're not knocked up, are you?' They don't make greeting cards for that occasion." He blew out a breath and raked his hand through his hair. "It doesn't mean I didn't worry about you, think about you. I did." *Endlessly.* "I still do."

"Well, now you can rest easy."

She hadn't a clue. He reined in the frustration. The fear was tougher. He wasn't sure he was going to survive watching her walk away from him again. "I'm glad you told me," he repeated.

She looked down. "I'm not." Her voice was a bare whisper.

He stepped closer, no longer caring about the risks. He couldn't hurt any worse. "You're not glad I know you're not pregnant?"

She looked up at him. Her eyes were glassy. She took a visible breath. "I'm not glad I'm not pregnant."

He felt as if she'd punched him in the heart. He fumbled, not wanting to say the wrong thing, scared to death to say he felt the same way. "After what happened last time—"

She shook her head. "It's not about the baby I lost. Miscarriages, as tragic and painful as the timing of mine was, aren't uncommon. My doctor told me it didn't decrease my chances of having another baby."

"Then what—"

She shut him up with a short shake of her head. She blew out a breath on a long sigh, then closed the distance between them. She took his hand. She was a toucher. That hadn't changed. Peace settled over him like a comforting blanket.

"I should have done that first."

She looked from their joined hands to his face. "Done what?"

"Touched you." He lifted a hand to her face. His fingers trembled as he stroked her soft skin. "Everything seems to make sense when I'm touching you."

"Then why did you stop?"

He didn't answer right away.

She finally closed her other hand over his and stopped him. "Why, John?"

"Maybe because I wasn't sure my touch would be enough. That *I* would be enough." His fingers lifted to weave through hers. He tightened them, still cupping her cheek. "I thought it would be easier not to try at all. To let you find what made you happy."

"And was it? Easier?"

"Not even close."

"Well, I tried to find happiness. I have a new job and a new condo and a new outlook on life."

"New outlook?"

"The one I decided on the day we made love. Remember what you said on Martinique, about risk? You said that what you get back in personal growth from standing up to what you fear most is at the very least equal to the risk you take. Well, that's my new motto. To make my own happiness. To risk everything and anything to get it, never to let myself stop believing it was worth it.

"But I knew my happiness wouldn't be complete until I saw you again. Except I was afraid to take that risk."

"What are you risking by seeing me?"

She shifted his hand to her chest. "My heart. It's been yours since some point on Martinique."

Stunned, he said nothing.

"I thought I could work it out on my own," she said. "You obviously had made your decision. But when I found out I wasn't pregnant, it hurt. A lot. And I knew I was crawling back into my safe hole again." She held his gaze. "Maybe Scottie understood that. Whatever the circumstances, here we are."

"I don't think I've ever respected anyone as much as I do you, Cali Ellis. Certainly not myself." This time he shook his head when she would have spoken. On a raw, choked whisper, he said, "It hurt me too."

She gasped softly, her hand clutched his. "What did?"

"That you weren't pregnant."

"Oh, John."

He wasn't sure who tugged whom, but they were both wrapped in each other's arms an instant later. His mouth found hers, and she opened for him willingly. He took all she was giving him, reveling in the discovery of what he'd been missing all along. "That magic circle, Cali. That's what I want. I want to make one." He lifted his head. "With you." He dropped a gentle kiss on her surprised, parted lips. "I have no idea how to do it. It scares me to death."

"You know what?" she whispered. "I want that too. With you." She kissed him, gently at first, but it quickly escalated until they were both grasping each other's arms just to stay upright.

John broke away first, pulling in a deep breath. "I love you, Cali Stanfield Ellis."

Eyes shining, she kissed him. "I love you, John McShane."

Heart pounding, but only with joy, he said, "How do you feel about adding another name to that list?"

"Cali Stanfield Ellis McShane?" She grinned. "Has sort of a magical ring to it, don't you think?"

"Yeah," he said roughly, catching her hard against him. "Yeah, it does."

She moved her head a fraction, making him pause a heartbeat away from her mouth. "What?"

"I'm adding a name to mine. Are you going to add a new job title to yours?"

"They want me as strategy coordinator, in-house."

She smiled. "Well, as the new resident code buster, that means we would probably have to work"—she snuggled more tightly against him—"very closely with each other."

"Why didn't you just say so?" She laughed, and his heart melted. He joined her, reeling from the power of the joy that flooded through him. He took her face in his hands. "Welcome to our magic circle," he whispered against her lips.

When he finally released her mouth long minutes later, she looked into his eyes and said, "Welcome home, John McShane."

THE EDITORS' CORNER

May Day! Cinco de Mayo! Mother's Day! Memorial Day! Armed Forces Day! Okay, okay, that last one's a stretch, but hey, the merry month of May is a time to celebrate. May signals the beginning of summer, National Barbecue Month, picnics, fairs, and don't forget, four excellent LOVESWEPTs knocking on the door. This month's quartet of love includes a stolen dog, a sleepwalker, a man with a smile that should be registered as a lethal weapon, and a woman who picks herbs in the nude! How's that for reading variety?

Take one U.S. marshal, a feisty P.I., an escaped convict, and a stolen poodle, and you've got a surefire way of learning the **TRICKS OF THE TRADE**, LOVESWEPT #834 by Cheryln Biggs. Mick Gentry and B.J. Poydras have no reason to know each other—after all, he's from Nevada and she's from

Louisiana. But the two are destined to meet when his case takes a nosedive straight into hers. The spunky detective prefers working alone, which is just fine with the rugged marshal, but when clues keep leading them to each other, can he convince her to put aside their differences long enough to give love a chance? Cheryln Biggs ignites a sizzling partnership that's hotter than a sultry summer night in the Big Easy!

When Duncan Glendower watches Andrea Lauderdale sleepwalk straight into his bed and into his arms, he realizes that he's a goner in Kathy Lynn Emerson's **SLEEPWALKING BEAUTY**, LOVE-SWEPT #835. Haunted by events that refuse to let her sleep in peace, Andrea reaches out to him in the darkness, tempting him to break all his rules. Struggling to protect the troubled beauty in a remote lodge, Duncan knows that sharing close quarters with the woman he's always loved is risky at best. But can he help Andrea fight the fears that rule her and prove to her that he'll never let her go? Kathy Lynn Emerson explores a man's desire to protect what's precious in this deeply moving novel of passion and possession.

Worried that the deadly threats against her small airport are somehow linked to the arrival of charter pilot Dillon Kinley, Sami Reed must decide if she dares to trust a sexy stranger who is **CHARMED AND DANGEROUS**, LOVESWEPT #836, by Jill Shalvis. Flashing a killer smile and harboring a score to settle, Dillon informs Sami that he won't be an easy tenant to please. But when fury turns to tenderness and old sorrows to new longings, can Sami win her rebel's love? New to LOVESWEPT, Jill Shalvis beguiles readers with a breathless tale of revenge and remembrance about the rogue whose caresses make his cool-eyed spitfire shameless.

In **MIDNIGHT REMEDY**, LOVESWEPT #837, Eve Gaddy brings together a lady with a slightly sinful past and a doctor who's traveled miles of bumpy road to reach her. Piper Stevenson has supposedly cured one of Dr. Eric Chambers's patients with a mystical remedy that she refuses to share. When Eric lights a fire in Piper's heart, will this nursery owner allow herself to come out of the darkness and into the lightness of love? Eve Gaddy reveals a delectably funny and yet touchingly poignant romance that renews faith in the heart and tells of a forgiveness strong enough to last forever.

Pssst! Not to spoil a surprise, but . . . keep an eye out for some changes on the LOVESWEPT horizon when we bring back a new, yet traditional look to our covers!

Happy reading!

With warmest wishes,

Shauna Summers

Joy Abella

Shauna Summers   Joy Abella

Editor   Administrative Editor

Don't miss these extraordinary
women's fiction titles by your
favorite Bantam authors

On sale in March:

A THIN DARK LINE
by *Tami Hoag*

THE BRIDE'S BODYGUARD
by *Elizabeth Thornton*

PLACES BY THE SEA
by *Jean Stone*

*When a sadistic act of violence
leaves a woman dead . . .
When a tainted piece of evidence
lets her killer walk . . .
How far would you go to see justive done?*

A THIN DARK LINE

the new hardcover thriller
by *New York Times* bestselling author

Tami Hoag

*When murder erupts in a small Southern town, Tami
Hoag leads readers on a frightening journey to the shadowy
boundary between attraction and obsession, law and justice—and exposes the rage that lures people over a thin
dark line.*

*Her body lay on the floor. Her slender arms outflung,
palms up. Death. Cold and brutal, strangely intimate.*

The people rose in unison as the judge emerged
from his chambers. The Honorable Franklin
Monahan. The figurehead of justice. The decision
would be his.

*Black pools of blood in the silver moonlight. Her life
drained from her to puddle on the hard cypress floor.*

Richard Kudrow, the defense attorney. Thin,
gray, and stoop-shouldered, as if the fervor for justice
had burned away all excess within him and had begun
to consume muscle mass. Sharp eyes and the strength
of his voice belied the image of frailty.

Her naked body inscribed with the point of a knife. A work of violent art.

Smith Pritchett, the district attorney. Sturdy and aristocratic. The gold of his cufflinks catching the light as he raised his hands in supplication.

Cries for mercy smothered by the cold shadow of death.

Chaos and outrage rolled through the crowd in a wave of sound as Monahan pronounced his ruling. The small amethyst ring had not been listed on the search warrant of the defendant's home and was, therefore, beyond the scope of the warrant and not legally subject to seizure.

Pamela Bichon, thirty-seven, separated, mother of a nine-year-old girl. Brutally murdered. Eviscerated. Her naked body found in a vacant house on Pony Bayou, spikes driven through the palms of her hands into the wood floor; her sightless eyes staring up at nothing through the slits of a feather Murdi Gras mask.

Case dismissed.

The crowd spilled from the Partout Parish courthouse, past the thick Doric columns and down the broad steps, a buzzing swarm of humanity centering on the key figures of the drama that had played out in Judge Monahan's courtroom.

Smith Pritchett focused his narrow gaze on the dark blue Lincoln that awaited him at the curb and snapped off a staccato line of "no comments" to the frenzied press. Richard Kudrow, however, stopped his descent dead center on the steps.

Trouble was the word that came immediately to Annie Broussard as the press began to ring themselves around the defense attorney and his client. Like every other deputy in the sheriff's office, she had hoped against hope that Kudrow would fail in his attempt to get the ring thrown out as evidence. They had all hoped Smith Pritchett would be the one crowing on the courthouse steps.

Sergeant Hooker's voice crackled over the portable radio. "Savoy, Mullen, Prejean, Broussard, move in front of those goddamn reporters. Establish some distance between the crowd and Kudrow and Renard before this turns into a goddamn cluster fuck."

Annie edged her way between bodies, her hand resting on the butt of her baton, her eyes on Renard as Kudrow began to speak. He stood beside his attorney looking uncomfortable with the attention being focused on him. He wasn't a man to draw notice. Quiet, unassuming, an architect in the firm of Bowen & Briggs. Not ugly, not handsome. Thinning brown hair neatly combed and hazel eyes that seemed a little too big for their sockets. He stood with his shoulders stooped and his chest sunken, a younger shadow of his attorney. His mother stood on the step above him, a thin woman with a startled expression and a mouth as tight and straight as a hyphen.

"Some people will call this ruling a travesty of justice," Kudrow said loudly. "The only travesty of justice here has been perpetrated by the Partout Parish sheriff's department. Their *investigation* of my client has been nothing short of harassment. Two proir searches of Mr. Renard's home produced nothing that might tie him to the murder of Pamela Bichon."

"Are you suggesting the sheriff's department manipuilated evidence?" a reporter called out.

"Mr. Renard has been the victim of a narrow and fanatical investigation led by Detective Nick Fourcade. Y'all are aware of Fourcade's record with the New Orleans police department, of the reputation he brought with him to this parish. Detective Fourcade *allegedly* found that ring in my client's home. Draw you own conclusions."

As she elbowed past a television cameraman, Annie could see Fourcade turning around, half a dozen steps down from Kudrow. The cameras focused on him hastily. His expression was a stone mask, his eyes hidden by a pair of mirrored sunglasses. A cigarette smoldered between his lips. His temper was a thing of legend. Rumors abounded through the department that he was not quite sane.

He said nothing in answer to Kudrow's insinuation, and yet the air between them seemed to thicken. Anticipation held the crowd's breath. Fourcade pulled the cigarette from his mouth and flung it down, exhaling smoke through his nostrils. Annie took a half step toward Kudrow, her fingers curling around the grip of her baton. In the next heartbeat Fourcade was bounding up the steps—straight at Marcus Renard, shouting, "NO!"

"He'll kill him!" someone shrieked.

"Fourcade!" Hooker's voice boomed as the fat sergeant lunged after him, grabbing at and missing the back of his shirt.

"You killed her! You killed my baby girl!"

The anguished shouts tore from the throat of Hunter Davidson, Pamela Bichon's father, as he hurled himself down the steps at Renard, his eyes rolling, one arm swinging wildly, the other hand clutching a .45.

Fourcade knocked Renard aside with a beefy shoulder, grabbed Davidson's wrist and shoved it skyward as the .45 barked out a shot and screams went up all around. Annie hit Davidson from the right side, her much smaller body colliding with his just as Fourcade threw his weight against the man from the left. Davidson's knees buckled and they all went down in a tangle of arms and legs, grunting and shouting, bouncing hard down the steps, Annie at the bottom of the heap. Her breath was pounded out of her as she hit the concrete steps with four-hundred pounds of men on top of her.

"He killed her!" Hunter Davidson sobbed, his big body going limp. "He butchered my girl!"

Annie wriggled out from under him and sat up, grimacing. All she could think was that no physical pain could compare with what this man must have been enduring.

Swiping back the strands of dark hair that had pulled loose from her ponytail, she gingerly brushed over the throbbing knot on the back of her head. Her fingertips came away sticky with blood.

"Take this," Fourcade ordered in a low voice, thrusting Davidson's gun at Annie butt-first. Frowning, he leaned down over Davidson and put a hand on the man's shoulder even as Prejean snapped the cuffs on him. "I'm sorry," he murmured. "I wish I could'a let you kill him."

The author of the national bestseller *Dangerous to Hold* once again combines intoxicating passion with spellbinding suspense . . .

He'd sworn to protect her with his life.

THE BRIDE'S BODYGUARD
BY ELIZABETH THORTON

"A major, major talent . . . [a] superstar."—*Rave Reviews*

With his striking good looks, Ross Trevenan was one of the most attractive men Tessa Lorimer had ever seen. But five minutes in his company convinced her he was the most arrogant, infuriating man alive. That's why it was such a shock to discover Trevenan's true purpose: hired to escort her out of Paris and back to England, he had sworn that he'd do anything to keep her safe—even if he had to marry her to do it. Now, finding herself a bride to a devastatingly attractive bodyguard seems more hazardous than any other situation she could possibly encounter. Yet Tessa doesn't know that she holds the key to a mystery that Trevenan would sell his soul to solve . . . and a vicious murderer would kill to keep.

A movement on the terrace alerted Ross to the presence of someone else.

"Paul?"

Tessa's voice. Ross threw his cheroot on the ground and crushed it under his heel.

"Paul?" Her voice was breathless, uncertain. "I saw you from my window. I wasn't sure it was you until I saw our signal."

Ross said nothing, but he'd already calculated that he'd stumbled upon the trysting place of Tessa and her French lover and had inadvertently given their signal merely by smoking a cheroot.

Tessa entered the gazebo and halted, waiting for her eyes to become accustomed to the gloom. "Paul, stop playing games with me. You know you want to kiss me."

It never crossed Ross's mind to enlighten her about his identity. He was too curious to see how far the brazen hussy would go.

Her hands found his shoulders. "Paul," she whispered, and she lifted her head for his kiss.

It was exactly as she had anticipated. His mouth was firm and hot, and those pleasant sensations began to warm her blood. When he wrapped his arms around her and jerked her hard against his full length, she gave a little start of surprise, but that warm, mobile mouth on hers insisted she yield to him. She laughed softly when he kissed her throat, then she stopped breathing altogether when he bent her back and kissed her breasts, just above the lace on her bodice. He'd never gone that far before.

She should stop him, she knew she should stop him, but she felt as weak as a kitten. She said something—a protest? a plea?—and his mouth was on hers again, and everything Tessa knew about men and their passions was reduced to ashes in the scorching heat of that embrace. Her limbs were shaking, wild tremors shook her body, her blood seemed to ignite. She was clinging to him for support, kissing him back, allowing those bold hands of his to wander at will from her breast to her thigh, taking liberties she knew no decent girl should permit, not even a French girl.

When he left her mouth to kiss her ears, her eyebrows, her cheeks, she got out on a shaken whisper, "I never knew it could be like this. You make me feel things I never knew existed. You seem so different tonight."

And he did. His body was harder, his shoulders seemed broader, and she hadn't known he was so tall. As for his fragrance—

Then she knew, she *knew*, and she opened her eyes wide, trying to see his face. It was too dark, but she didn't need a light to know whose arms she was in. He didn't wear cologne as Paul did. He smelled of fresh air and soap and freshly starched linen.

"Trevenan!" she gasped, and fairly leapt out of his arms.

He made no move to stop her, but said in a laconic tone, "What a pity. And just when things were beginning to turn interesting."

She was so overcome with rage, she could hardly find her voice. "*Interesting?* What you did to me was not interesting. It was *depraved.*"

The lights on the terrace had yet to be extinguished, and she had a clear view of his expression. He could hardly keep a straight face.

"That's not the impression you gave me," he said. "I could have sworn you were enjoying yourself."

"I thought you were Paul," she shouted. "How dare you impose yourself on me in that hateful way."

He arched one brow. "My dear Miss Lorimer, as I recall, you were the one who imposed yourself on me. I was merely enjoying a quiet smoke when you barged into the gazebo and cornered me." His white teeth gleamed. "Might I give you a word of advice? You're too bold by half. A man likes to be the hunter. Try, if you can, to give the impression that *he* has cornered *you*."

She had to unclench her teeth to get the words out. "There is no excuse for your conduct. You knew I thought you were Paul."

"Come now. That trick is as old as Eve."

Anger made her forget her fear, and she took a quick step toward him. "Do you think I'd want your kisses? You're nothing but my grandfather's lackey. You're a secretary, an employee. If I were to tell him what happened here tonight," she pointed to the gazebo, "he would dismiss you."

"Tell him, by all means. He won't think less of me for acting like any red-blooded male. It's your conduct that will be a disappointment to him." His voice took on a hard edge. "By God, if I had the schooling of you, you'd learn to obey me."

"Thank God," she cried out, "that will never come to pass."

He laughed. "Stranger things have happened."

She breathed deeply, trying to find her calm. "If I'd known you were in the gazebo, I would never have entered it." His skeptical look revived her anger, and said, "I tell you, I thought you were Paul Marmont."

He shrugged. "In that case, all I can say is that little girls who play with fire deserve to get burned."

She raged, "You were teaching me a lesson?"

"In a word, yes."

Her head was flung back and she regarded him with smoldering dislike. "And just how far were you prepared to go in this lesson of yours, Mr. Trevenan? Mmm?"

He extended a hand to her, and without a trace of mockery or levity answered, "Come back to the gazebo with me and I'll show you."

In the bestselling tradition of Barbara Delinsky, an enthralling, emotionally charged novel of friendship, betrayal, forgiveness and love.

Jean Stone
PLACES BY THE SEA

Glamorous newswoman Jill McPhearson's past is calling her back . . . to an island, a house, a life she wants only to forget. Putting her childhood home on Martha's Vineyard in order takes all Jill's strength, but it will also give this savvy reporter her biggest break: the chance to go after the story of a lifetime . . . her own.

By the time she reached the end of Water Street, Jill realized where she had come. The lighthouse stood before her. The lighthouse where she'd spent so many hours, months, years, with Rita, thinking, dreaming, hoping.

She climbed down the dunes and found the path that led to their special place. Perhaps she'd find an answer here, perhaps she'd find some understanding as to what she had just read.

On the rocks, under the pier, what she found, instead, was Rita.

Jill stared at the back of the curly red hair. On the ground beside Rita stood a half-empty bottle of scotch. The ache in Jill's heart began to quiet, soothed by the comforting presence of her best friend—her once, a long time ago, best friend. She brushed her tears away and took another step.

"Care to share that bottle with an old friend?" she asked. "May I join you?"

Rita shrugged. "Last time I checked, it was still a free country."

Jill hesitated a moment. She didn't need Rita's caustic coldness right now. What she needed was a friend.

She hesitated a moment, then stooped beside her friend. "I thought maybe you'd be glad to see me."

Rita laughed. "Sorry. I was just too darned busy to roll out the red carpet."

Jill settled against a rock and faced Rita.

"Are you still angry at me for leaving the island?"

Rita stared off toward Chappy. "If I remember correctly, I left before you did."

"Where did you go, Rita? Why did you leave?"

Picking up the bottle of scotch, Rita took a swig. She held it a moment, then passed it to Jill without making eye contact. "Why did it surprise you that I left? You were the one who always said what a shithole this place was. You were the one who couldn't wait to get out of here."

Jill looked down the long neck of the bottle, then raised it to her lips. "But you were the one who wanted to stay."

Rita shrugged again. "Shit happens."

She handed the bottle back. "I've missed you."

A look of doubt bounced from Rita to Jill. "How long has it been? Twenty-five years? Well you missed me so much I never even got a Christmas card."

"My mother never told me you'd come back."

"That's no surprise. You should have guessed, though. You always thought I was destined to rot in this place."

Reaching out, Jill touched Rita's arm. Rita pulled away.

Jill took back her hand and rested it in her lap. "I was trying to make a new life for myself."

"And a fine job you did. So what is it now, Jill? Going to be another of the island's celebrities who graces us with your presence once a year?"

"No I'm selling the house."

Rita laughed. "See what I mean? You don't care about it here. You don't care about any of us. You never did."

A small wave lapped the shore. "Is that what you think?"

"You always thought I'd wind up like my mother. Well, in a lot of ways I guess I did. That should make you happy."

"Rita . . . I never meant . . . "

Rita's voice was slow, deliberate. "Yes you did. You were smarter than me, Jill. Prettier. More ambitious. I guess that's not a crime."

"It is if I hurt you that badly."

"You didn't hurt me, Jill. Pissed me off, maybe. But, no, you didn't hurt me."

Jill remembered Rita's laughter, Rita's toughness, and that Rita had always used these defenses to hide her insecurities, to hide her feelings that she wasn't as good as the kids who lived in the houses with mothers and fathers, the kids with dinner waiting on the table and clean, pressed clothes in their closets.

The heat of the sun warmed her face. "Life doesn't always go the way we want," she said. "No matter how hard we try."

Rita pulled her knees to her chest. "No shit."

The sound of a motor boat approached. They

both turned to watch as it shot through the water, white foam splashing, leaving a deep "V" of a wake.

"I can't believe you still come here," Jill said.

"Not many other places to think around here," Rita answered. "Especially in August." She hugged her knees, and looked at Jill. "I was real sorry about your parents. Your dad. Your mother."

"Thanks."

"I went to the service. For your mother."

Jill flicked her gaze back to the lighthouse, to the tourists. "I was in Russia," she said, aware that her words sounded weak, because Rita would know the real reason Jill hadn't returned had nothing to do with Russia. "Is your mother still . . ."

"Hazel?" Rita laughed. "Nothing's going to kill her. Found herself a man a few years ago. They live in Sarasota now."

Jill nodded. "That's nice. She's such a great person."

Rita plucked the bottle again and took another drink. "Yeah, well, she's different."

Closing her eyes, Jill let the sun soothe her skin, let herself find comfort in the sound of Rita's voice, in the way her words danced with a spirit all their own—a familiar, safe dance that Jill had missed for so long. "I've never had another best friend, Rita," she said, her eyes still closed to the sun, her heart opening to her friend.

Rita didn't reply.

Jill sat up and checked her watch. "I'd love to have you meet my kids," she said. "In fact, I have to pick up my daughter now." She hesitated a moment, then heard herself add, "Would you like to come?"

Rita paused for a heartbeat, or maybe it was two. "What time is it?"

"Five-thirty."

"I've got to start work at six. I tried to quit, but Charlie wouldn't let me. I'm a waitress there. At the tavern. Like my mother was."

"Tell Charlie he can live without you for one night," Jill said. "Come with me, Rita. Please."

Rita seemed to think about it. "What the hell," she finally said. "Why not."

The sun seemed to smile; the world seemed to come back into focus. "Great," Jill said, as she rose to her feet. "We've got so much to catch up on. First, though, we have to go back to my house and get the car. Amy's out at Gay Head."

"The car?" Rita asked.

Jill brushed off her shorts. "Hopefully, the workmen or any of their friends haven't boxed me in. I'm having some work done on the house and it's a power-saw nightmare."

"I'll tell you what," Rita said as she screwed the cap on the bottle. "You get the car. I'll wait here."

Jill didn't understand why Rita didn't want to come to the house, but, then Rita was Rita, and she always was independent. "Don't go away," she said as she waved good-bye and headed toward the road, realizing then that she hadn't asked Rita if she had ever married, or if she had any kids.

She was in the clear. At least about Kyle, Rita was in the clear.

She stared across the water and hugged her arms around herself. Jill had never known why Rita had left the Vineyard; she'd never known that Rita had been pregnant. Her secret was safe for now, safe forever.

And Jesus, it felt good to have a friend again.

On sale in April:

MISCHIEF

by Amanda Quick

ONCE A WARRIOR

by Karyn Monk